THE DANGEROUS ILLUSION OF ART

D1553929

The Sequel to *Blood and Faith* and BOOK TWO in the
LAURA COLE ADVENTURES SERIES

The DANGEROUS ILLUSION of ART

a novel

JOHN FROHNMAYER

LUMINARE PRESS
WWW.LUMINAREPRESS.COM

Printed in the United States of America

WWW.JOHNFROHNMAYER.COM

Luminare Press
442 Charnelton St.
Eugene, OR 97401
www.luminarepress.com

LCCN: 2023914785
ISBN: 979-8-88679-349-9

For my sister Mira.

Also by John Frohnmayer

Leaving Town Alive:
Confessions of an Arts Warrior

Out of Tune:
Listening to the First Amendment

Socrates the Rower:
How Rowing Informs Philosophy

Sunriver: A Legacy

Carrying the Clubs:
What Golf Teaches Us About Ethics

Skiing and the Poetry of Snow

SPIN! (Musical Comedy with Sila Shaman)

Blood and Faith
(Book One in the Lara Cole Adventures Series)

TABLE OF CONTENTS

CHAPTER 1

The obstacle is the path.

Museum director Lara Cole was sitting at her desk at Akerhill, in Northern Virginia, getting nothing done. Grief had engulfed her in the six months since she had flown home from Russia on a US Air Force transport, spending the entire flight sitting beside Michael's casket. She was trying to be tough, telling herself that Michael's love would always be with her, giving her strength.

It wasn't working. Grief, like a black shroud, lay upon the frame of her life.

The phone rang. She stared at it dumbly. It was Randall Martin, chairman of the National Endowment for the Arts. Randall, notwithstanding his lofty position in the art world, belonged to the kung fu school of social graces, and without preliminary said:

"Look, I know Michael got shot and you saw him die, but you can't curl up like a salted slug. You've got a life to live and I have a plan to help you move along. I want you to do a site visit out west."

Lara got up from her desk, cradled the cordless phone against her neck and shoulder, shook out the cuff of her tan linen slacks, and began to pace. She had a temper and the heat in her skull fried out the grief.

"You know what, Randall? You really piss me off. You always have." She and Randall had known each other since college.

"Thank you, Lara. It is what I do best, but here is the deal: we gave an advancement grant for a total of $250,000 to a museum out in Nowheresville, Oregon…"

"It is pronounced Orygun, you idiot."

"Whatever. Half of the grant amount has been disbursed and things were cooking along with interim reports and all that crapola until the board, or somebody out there, up and fired the director. And then half the board resigned, and the state attorney general started an investigation under their oversight of nonprofit corporations, and all of a sudden everything is a foot deep in doo-doo."

"Why me?"

"Because you are the Failure Queen. You have experience running an arts organization that is totally screwed up. That's why."

"Up yours, Randall." She pegged the phone into the couch like a catcher picking off a runner at second. The phone, sustaining no serious damage, started ringing immediately. She let it ring until it stopped. Then it started ringing again and she picked it up, but didn't say anything.

"Look, Lara, I wouldn't ask you to do this site visit if I did not hold you in the highest regard. You are the smartest, the bravest, and the prettiest failed museum director I know, and I greatly value your judgment gained from a rash of unfortunate experiences."

"Randall, normally I would climb through this phone line and strangle your fat neck, but today I am too tender to put up with any of your bullshit." She threw the phone again, this time bouncing it off the couch, and onto the floor where it separated into three pieces.

The phone at her secretary's desk began to buzz. She ignored it.

———◆———

RANDALL PERSISTED FOR THE NEXT FEW DAYS, AND having little else to do since Akerhill Museum was struggling, with its founder dead and its reputation in disarray, Lara relented. The year was 1996.

The National Endowment for the Arts is one of America's cultural agencies tasked by congressional legislation to support the arts nationwide with grants and programs. Site visitors (sometimes known as seagulls—they fly in, flap and squawk and shit, and fly away) are supposed to be experienced professionals who can observe the progress of a grantee, make evaluations, and give advice that is, hopefully, helpful. The goal is not just to examine how the money is being spent, but to ensure the success of the project in accordance with the details of the grant application and the expectations of the granting agency.

Institutions that are "visited" are not always thrilled to host the interloper. An imperious grand inquisitor, with a portfolio from the Council of Trent, sucks away resources from the institution being examined, and the very notion that an outsider could swoop in and evaluate accurately within a couple of days, let alone make helpful suggestions, defies both logic and experience. On the other hand, if the institution is not playing by the rules or is otherwise in danger of not being able to fulfil its grant obligations, a site visitor makes a lot of sense.

But Lara was not greeted with either skepticism or relief when she arrived.

She was not greeted at all.

The museum doors were locked, and none of the contact numbers she had been given answered.

———————◆————————

RANDALL MARTIN, CHAIRMAN OF THE NATIONAL Endowment for the Arts in Washington, DC, had studied classics in college and thus was familiar with ancient mythology. He described his job as Sisyphean: diversity of American culture was the hill, disinterest and outright hostility the rock, and lack of money the friction as it rolled back down the hill. For every grant the agency gave, it created one ingrate and ninety-nine disappointed bitchers. But Randall soldiered on, quoting Churchill (whom he resembled in rotundity only) by preaching that success is going from failure to failure without loss of enthusiasm.

Lara Cole, 35 and single, or rather divorced, but so long ago it didn't really count, was director of Akerhill Museum in Virginia and had been host to a Russian icon that was stolen amid much drama and mayhem. In the world of art, she was famous—like Typhoid Mary. Previously she had worked for Sotheby's in London and the Metropolitan Museum in New York and had plenty of credentials. She was tough, smart, and blessed/cursed with an unquiet mind, short, dark hair, and the body of an athlete.

After she got past Randall's tasteless presentation, she looked upon the invitation to go out to Oregon for a few days as a welcome diversion. It would prove to be much more than that.

The building looked like a house. A very large house with lots of glass and low walls and a horizontal flow. Maybe a Frank Lloyd Wright wannabe with lots of money built it, but it had a brass plate that said Left Coast Cultural Center, and that was her destination. Repeated ringing of the bell brought no one, not even a guard.

Lara walked back into the parking lot and studied the huge building. It looked like the prow of a ship incongruously beached among the ponderosa pines. The long overhang sheltered a patio with a reflecting pool that doubled the geometry of the seemingly unsupported structure. The place can't be abandoned, she thought. But how the hell am I supposed to make contact? She fished out the letter from Randall's office that contained her marching orders. Linda McKenzie was the "acting director." It was her number that brought no response.

The town Randall had called Nowheresville actually had a name: Salish. Lara didn't know who or what a Salish was, but there was no information to be gained here in the lonesome pines, so she got into her rental car and headed for Salish.

She was underwhelmed. Salish consisted of two blocks of dilapidated buildings, a tavern, and a Forest Service headquarters and repair shop. A few residential streets, unpaved two-block dead ends, and the obligatory mix of mobiles, cinderblock bungalows, and modest clapboards completed the census. Not even a goddamned gas station.

She went into the Forest Service office.

"Well, aren't you a pretty lady?"

Great start, thought Lara.

"Sir, I am trying to find somebody at the Left Coast Cultural Center, but the place is locked up, and I can't reach anyone on the phone."

"A weird place, that," he said. His nameplate said John Rawlings. "I have been livin' in these parts for thirty years and never have I seen so much money thrown down the rathole as at that place. You look at the stuff they hang on the walls and I swear my granddaughter could do better, and she is only six."

"Would you know, please, how I could get in touch with somebody who is in charge there?"

"And they invite all manner of drum bangers and moccasin stompers and other hangers-on to powwows or whatever they call 'em, and they get themselves all worked up over stuff that just makes no livin' sense."

"Umm, Mr. Rawlings, I am not here to debate the virtues of the center. I really would appreciate it if you could help me contact somebody there."

"Just have a seat, pretty lady, and I will call the wife. She knows more about that highfalutin' stuff than I do."

She sat.

The conversation with "the wife," at least the part Lara could hear, consisted of lots of uh-huhs, don't know 'ems, and not on my radars, but when he hung up he gave Lara two names and phone numbers: Mary Kass and Frank Bolinger. Progress, maybe.

Lara thanked him, got a "You're welcome, Sweetie" in return, and went back to her car. It was getting dark, and Lara had no idea where she was going to eat, sleep, or be until she rousted out somebody affiliated with the locked-tight arts center.

She went back into the Forest Service office and said: "Mister Rawlings, is there anywhere to stay here in Salish?" His leer told her immediately that his response would register on the dipshit scale.

"Ah, I knew you couldn't resist me. I slay the ladies, that I do."

Lara had had enough; her temper took over. "Cut the crap, Buster. I asked you a polite question, and I expect you to lay off the sexist bullshit and give me a polite reply."

He was legitimately surprised. Not that anything about his behavior was legitimate. He just wasn't used to young females getting in his face, and he actually blushed.

"I'm sorry, I meant no harm. I was just tryin' to be friendly."

"Apology accepted. Now is there a motel in town?"

"Well, it ain't exactly a motel. It hasn't got a sign, but there are four or five rooms that this guy rents, and once you have given him your credit card he tells you the code that opens the door. Never been in there, but it is the only show in town."

"Got the number?" He had.

"How about food?"

"One choice, but it is the oldest continually functioning tavern in Oregon, and it is a half block from where you will be staying, if it suits you."

Lara wasn't a snob about where she stayed. Her father, on road trips in the family sedan, always knew "a better place down the road," and they ended up in some incredible dives. It was his idea of a joke, just like his ability to fart on demand as he walked around in his pajamas watering the lawn on summer mornings.

The code worked, and the room was presentable, clean, and had some original watercolors and prints on the wall—a rarity in Lara's experience where most transient rooms were decorated with crap that cost more than legitimate art done by legitimate artists. The building was on the main drag, had a couple of chairs on the porch where one could sit and watch the log trucks go by, and next to the parking space was the world's shortest river that came out of a pipe, flowed freely for twenty feet, and disappeared under the highway. Oregon Rural Renaissance at its finest.

FOOD. SHE WASHED HER FACE, THOUGHT ABOUT CALLING the names she had been given, but decided to wait until tomorrow, and walked to the tavern. There she learned that the mahogany bar had come around the horn by sailing ship, that the name Salish referred to the root language of many Northwest tribes, that the pizza was fine, and the beer was from a micro-brewery in Roseburg, the closest city. It was everything she needed to cap off a day in which she had accomplished nothing.

CHAPTER 2

The yawn of an embarrassed dog.

Mary Kass, first on Lara's list of two, didn't answer. Frank Bolinger did, but he was busy in his hardware store and asked her if she could meet him for a sandwich about noon. He would have to stay at the store, but if she could bring along something for herself, they could talk while he kept an eye out for customers. Roseburg was west of Salish; she had driven through it on the way here so she knew the road—a pretty drive, first through rolling oak savannah, then through the fir and pine forest with occasional stretches along the Umpqua River and glimpses of the Cascade volcanoes.

She had plenty of time to…to…to do, what? She decided to check out Roseburg, so she drove to town and found a visitor information center. There she learned that Roseburg's history was explosive—literally. Explosions were all over the news since Timothy McVeigh had just blown up the Federal Building in Oklahoma City, but this one in Roseburg, about 35 years before, was accidental. A truck driver arrived too late to unload, so he parked his truck next to a hardware store and got a room for the night. A fire broke out in a trash can around midnight, and ten minutes after the firefighters arrived, the truck, loaded with 13,000 pounds of dynamite and ammonium nitrate, blew up, killing fourteen and leveling an eight-block area of the downtown. It blew a police officer who was twenty blocks away out of his chair. Houses on the hill had their plate glass windows pinned in shards on the opposite wall like a devil's dartboard. A hotel guest was blown out of his room and into the hall. Estimate: $12 million in damage along with a crater fifty-two feet wide and twenty feet deep.

Lara learned this from the nice lady at the visitor center along with the news that Aaron Rose had founded the town in 1851 and no, the Rose Festival was not here, but three hours north in Portland. When she got to Frank Bolinger's hardware store she asked if his was the store that blew. It wasn't, but the store that was demolished was still in business—at a different location, obviously—and was a friendly competitor.

Lara sat down at a small table to the side of the cash register and unwrapped her sandwich. Bolinger was somewhere between fifty and seventy—hard to tell. He had dark hair, but his face was weathered, his manner mild. When he got up to help a customer, she was surprised at his height; he was all legs with a short torso.

"As I explained on the phone, I am trying to contact someone who can tell me about what is going on at the Left Coast Cultural Center."

"Good luck on that one. I am a trustee, and I sure as hell don't know."

"You are a trustee. Isn't it your job to know stuff—isn't that what a trustee does?"

"Was a trustee. I run a hardware store and try to be a good citizen. That is why I joined the board. I can read a balance sheet and a profit and loss statement and give advice on business matters, but I don't know much about art and culture, and that is what the center is really about."

"Tell me as much as you know about what has happened."

"First you tell me. Am I going to get in trouble here? Should I be calling my lawyer?"

"Mr. Bolinger, I am not in law enforcement. I am a museum director here on behalf of the National Endowment for the Arts, which gave a $250,000 advancement grant to the center, and they want to make sure their money is being well spent. As you probably know, advancement grants are among the largest that the endowment gives. They are very competitive, and it is a real tribute to the work of your center to have gotten one. The point of the grant is to reward artistic excellence and move the institution to the next level of achievement."

"Well I know about the grant, and I can assure you that we keep good books. But you didn't answer my question: Am I in jeopardy here, and should I be calling my lawyer?"

"I know so little at this point that I cannot answer your question, but if you kept good books and paid attention to business, I can't see how you, personally, would be in jeopardy. I am not a lawyer, though."

"Thank the Lord for small favors," he said. "And, we did most of it right, I think."

"I sense a great big 'but' lurking in the air."

"Correct. The place has fallen apart."

"Aaah, that answer is a bit too cryptic. Tell me more."

"The director or CEO or whatever his title was, was Josh Bendix. He had been here for about five years and was, in my opinion, doing a fine job. He acquired some top-notch art and brought in some great programs. He was the one who argued for the NEA grant to 'take us to the next level.'

He was ambitious, but a good administrator—smart and good with people."

"What kind of art does the center have?" asked Lara.

"You are asking the wrong guy, but from what I know, some well-regarded Northwest artists, quite a few Native American objects, and a lot of Russian stuff, some of which I found really difficult."

"So, you were telling me what happened," prompted Lara.

"Then I missed a meeting of the trustees and the next thing I know Josh has been fired. About half the board that was at the meeting resigned, and the chair of the trustees appointed Linda McKenzie as acting director. Linda hadn't been here long; she was young—just out of school. Then Linda disappeared. Nobody seems to know where she went or what happened to her. The remaining trustees…well, I am guessing here because I don't really know, but somebody decided to close the place up. I had resigned before that, as had a couple of others, so I don't know who is left. The chair is probably the one to talk to. That's Piper Williams. She's the wife of Bill Williams of Williams Lumber."

"Jesus." Lara was stunned. "So nobody is in charge, the place is locked up, and you can't tell me what happened?"

"I've told you what I know. Talk to Piper—she can tell you more. Just a word, and I am not talking out of school here because everyone who knows her will tell you the same, she is very definite."

Lara didn't want to talk to Piper Williams on the phone. She wanted to look her in the eye and take the measure of the woman since she was the one who apparently was pulling the strings of the Left Coast Cultural Center. Bolinger had told Lara where to find her—a great big Victorian mansion suitable for the wife of a timber baron. Lara rang the bell. A butler answered, an honest to god English butler, dressed in a suit, chin elevated, shoes gleaming. A butler in Roseburg, Oregon. Beyond pretentious.

He asked if he could help her, and she told him he could. He would go and inquire whether Mrs. Williams was "available." He invited Lara to wait outside the door, which he politely closed.

He returned after a long enough interval that Lara had considered ringing the bell again. Mrs. Williams would like to know "the nature of your business" was what he said, and Lara told him. He nodded, closed the door in her face, but politely, and was gone for another interval. Lara knew when rude was being laid on her and so when he returned to say that Mrs. Williams was "indisposed," she was not surprised. Just pissed off.

———◆——

She called Randall at the NEA, explained that she couldn't get into the Cultural Center, and the only person who apparently knew what was going on refused to talk to her. Randall told her he would check with the NEA's general counsel (lawyer in non-governmentese) and would get back to her.

So that left Lara in another day with nothing to do unless she could find somebody else with local knowledge. She tried Mary Kass again, and this time got an answer and an invitation to come over for coffee. Progress.

Mary Kass sold real estate. Parked in her driveway was a black Mercedes 550 sedan. Apparently the clientele she served was first cabin. But she was nice and friendly and even slightly helpful. A little bit. She was blonde, vivacious, and mid-forties with several big diamonds on appropriate fingers. The coffee was good.

Cookies, too.

"What you've got to understand, Lara, is that Bill Williams is the pope here in Roseburg. He owns the biggest mill, the lumber and construction goods retail stores, all but Home Depot, and they can't even compete because Bill has bought up all the privately owned timberland and can undersell even the national chains. But money is only part of the picture. He knows every politician, every lawyer, every business leader. He is generous, gives away lots of money, and, although you might not expect it, is humble and a hell of a nice guy.

"His wife, Piper, on the other hand, were she a man, would be an asshole. Women can't be assholes, I guess— maybe rectum-ettes? Anyway, she is beyond difficult, very opinionated, abrupt, entitled, and demanding. She is chair of the Board of Trustees of the Cultural Center, and she runs it as if it were her own private fiefdom, which, in a way it is because husband Bill provided all of the materials and much of the money that built it. She could care less what anyone else thinks, and as far as she is concerned, rules are for other people. He, by the way, adores her; dotes on her. In his eyes she can do no wrong.

"I have been on the board for six years. It is good for my business since selling real estate, particularly in this small market, is all about who you know. But I couldn't take it anymore when she canned Josh Bendix. She didn't give any reason. She just said she had lost confidence in him and without even taking a vote of the board, she announced that she had handed him his hat. I, and four others, said we could no longer sit on a board where we were not involved in the decision-making. Piper didn't give a shit; she didn't even say goodbye, let alone thank us for our work.

"She then appointed Linda McKenzie as 'acting director.' Linda is a sweet girl, but she is no match for Piper and is so far out of her depth in trying to run the place that none of us wanted to be responsible for oversight, and so a couple more trustees quit. I really don't know who is left."

"I heard that no one can find Linda McKenzie," said Lara.

"Right. She is gone. Disappeared. Vanished. POOF!"

"Does anyone suspect foul play?" asked Lara, feeling as if she were playing the role of Dr. Watson.

"I don't think so. She lived alone and hadn't been on staff for long. I don't remember much about her background since Josh hired her. I really don't think anyone is looking; I mean it isn't like anyone has filed a missing person report."

"How do I get into the building?" asked Lara. "I am here to review the books and account for how the advancement grant money is being spent."

Mary shook her head. "You will have to talk to Piper, I am sorry to say. None of us who were on the board ever had keys, and if we did, we would be trespassers now. Have you talked to Piper?"

"I rang the bell and met the butler, but he reported that she was 'indisposed.'"

Mary rolled her eyes. "She will see you if she wants something. Otherwise, you are going to whistle for it."

"I am told by the NEA that the state Attorney General's Office is involved."

"That's news to me," said Mary.

Lara thanked her, accepted a cookie to go, and left.

CHAPTER 3

The peasants crave only circuses and bread.

———◆———

Lara thought she would test Piper Williams's indisposition, so she returned to the Victorian mansion, through the iron gates and English rose garden to the front door, and rang the bell.

The butler responded. He didn't exactly scowl at seeing Lara, but he lowered his chin ever so slightly, as if to say, "We don't cotton to the riffraff here, and you should make yourself gone."

"I would like to see Mrs. Williams now. My name is still Lara Cole, and I am here on behalf of the federal government." That was kind of true since the NEA is part of the federal government.

He departed.

She waited.

He returned to report that Mrs. Williams was not prepared to see her today or any other time. "Good day, to you."

Lara was ready for this and before he could close the door (politely meant slow, to his disadvantage), she thrust a note into his hand. It said:

Mrs. Williams,

I have been hired by the National Endowment for the Arts to perform a site visit of the Left Coast Cultural Center to review how the Advancement Grant of $250,000 is being spent. The center is contractually obligated to cooperate with this review. Since the center is closed, you are the only person who seems to have knowledge of its status and finances. I insist that you cooperate with me in performing my tasks.

I am carrying one of those new portable phones that is about the size of a brick. The number is 202-346-6676. I will return this afternoon at 4 pm to attempt to talk with you. If that time is not convenient, please call to arrange another time.

I appreciate your cooperation.

Lara Cole

LARA FELT THE CLUMSY CREAM-COLORED MOBILE PHONE. It was hot. She was not at all sure she liked having a phone with her all the time. There were times when being out of reach was kind to the mind. This was not one of those times, though, and as she was thinking, the phone rang. Could Piper Williams have responded so quickly? No, it was the general counsel of the NEA, a sweet and competent guy named Peter French, which—Lara was to learn—was the same name as an early Oregon rancher, land grabber, and builder of architecturally wonderful round barns.

"Peter, hi. Nice to hear from you."

"Lara, you, too. Randall tells me you can't get into the place. That's weird."

"It's locked up, and not even a guard is around. It is just sitting out there in the forest like a forgotten fairytale, and the only person who apparently knows anything, the wife of the local timber baron, won't see me."

"I can honestly say I haven't ever run into this situation before. Usually, grantees are falling all over themselves to prove they are worthy."

"What can you do to put a burr under her saddle?" Lara said, absorbing her western surroundings. If she got an outfit, she could be a cowboy, too.

"I will write her a letter and say in no uncertain terms that if she and the center don't fully cooperate with you, we will suspend any further payout on the grant and will take whatever action is necessary to get back the money we have already sent. I will fax it to them within the hour."

"That's great, but there is nobody home in the center to receive the fax."

"Give me the name of the lady who is the chair of the trustees. I will fax it to her as well."

"Peter, why don't you also fax a copy to Bill Williams, her husband, at the headquarters of Williams Lumber. I think she is going to avoid us as long as she can."

"Will do."

<hr />

LARA RETURNED TO THE VICTORIAN MANSION AT 4 PM, rang the bell, waited, rang the bell again, waited some more, and just for the hell of it, pressed the bell a third time and kept her finger on it for a full thirty seconds (she was timing it with her watch). No response.

Having nothing further to fail to accomplish, Lara drove around Roseburg. The town was bisected by the Interstate 5 freeway with most of the older part on the east side. She scoped out the courthouse, the VA Domiciliary, and various strip malls, and went into a tavern that could properly be called a clean, presentable dive. It was about 5:30 pm and a crowd (ten was a crowd around here) of locals were gathering around a small stage where a guy—in a business suit no less—was setting up with a speaker, stool, and guitar.

She took a table toward the back and ordered a beer. The "entertainer" had shed his suit coat, loosened his tie, and rolled up his sleeves. Lara wondered if she would have to leave her beer and race when the horrible off-key cowboy songs began. He made a few self-deprecating remarks to the mostly young females gathered around the stage. They clearly were fans and laughed appreciatively. Then he began to sing and play and, JESUS, he could do both. His voice was clear and light, his delivery intimate and, let's face it, sexy as hell. Lara was smitten—he had her halfway through the first song. She listened—rapt—her beer forgotten as he cruised through some James Taylor, some Roberta Flack, some Jackson Browne. She was in the back of the room, but his eyes captured her, sucked her in, told her that every song was for her alone. Time was suspended; her senses eclipsed.

She shook herself back to reality like a wet dog, left her beer, and got up to leave. He followed her with his eyes and nodded mid-song. She fled as if she had totally exposed herself to an utter stranger. As she unlocked her car, she pondered the experience that she could only describe as wonderfully unsettling. She had, in her mind, resolved to love Michael forever. Was she being untrue to his memory; fickle to her own emotions?

She was hungry and headed back to Salish. The hills of the oak savannah were steep and rolling, but as the road climbed, the trees changed from widespread broadleaf to evergreen, and at a certain elevation, ponderosas began to appear with their distinctive reddish bark. They and the lodgepole pines seemed to cohabitate with an occasional smooth-barked tree, also reddish, that Lara learned was a madrone. The sunlight through the trees flashed into shade like a projector illuminating a screen. She slowed down. It was damn hard to see, and she didn't want to hit a deer.

THE ROOM WAS NO BETTER BUT NO WORSE THAN SHE HAD left it. The bed was unmade, the towels rumpled and wet, and the small can of Folgers where she had found it. Room service, or even a maid to tidy up, were clearly not part of the deal. But that was okay because the tavern was still close by.

She sat at the bar this time, the one that had traveled around the horn, and chatted up the barman. He recommended Dead Guy Ale, made by Rogue Brewery, an Oregon ginmill over at the coast in Newport (every coastal state has a Newport). And to eat? Since Lara had had pizza last night and she couldn't handle pizza more than once a month, she ordered a smash-burger, which she was assured, was a house favorite.

"Smash-burger and Rogue Brewery and Dead Guy Ale," said Lara. "This sounds like a dangerous place." It wasn't busy and the bartender had time to chat.

"Just wait until the local yahoos get a few snorts in them and start playing word games or talking about Bigfoot sightings."

"Do you believe that, I mean about Bigfoot?" asked Lara.

"I tell myself no, and then find I am looking over my shoulder every time I am in the forest at dusk, wondering if I am going to see a hairy, eight-foot-tall creature striding across a logging road leaving footprints eighteen inches long. It is the kind of thing I want to believe because it would be so incredibly interesting to find a species science hasn't acknowledged."

"What else goes on in Salish; how do you folks entertain yourselves?"

"You are sitting in the cultural center of the metropolis of Salish. We come here to talk, to play cards, to flirt, and of course to drink. Most of us have jobs that are related to the forest somehow—you know, timber cruisers, firefighters, road builders—that sort of thing."

"What about the Left Coast Cultural Center?"

"What about it?"

"Well isn't it a big deal, a place that has great art and lots of interesting programs?" Lara was surprised at his facile dismissal of what she thought would be a pivotal part of community life.

"Most of my friends don't go there much. Occasionally they have a dance or some jazz, but I think that most of the people that go there come from outside the area. I am not a hick, but what they do there is pretty snooty."

Lara nodded her head in a noncommittal but witty fashion.

"Tell you what you might be interested in if you are around here for a bit. There is this crazy lady who lives in a dump a couple of blocks from here. She collects all sorts of crap, but some of it might be interesting to somebody like yourself who knows about art."

Yeah sure, thought Lara. Going through some crazy lady's junk sounds like a good time.

THE NEXT MORNING LARA GOT UP, PUT ON HER TIGHTS and running shoes, a fleece, and a hat, and set out for a run. Starting out at her usual eight-minute/mile pace, she got about four blocks and was sucking air. It wasn't the ale or the smash-burger, all of which went down without incident. Altitude. This place must be high. She turned up a dirt road into the forest, settled into an easy pace, and tried to let her mind just travel on at its own direction. But she found herself looking around, not hypervigilant, but just looking around in case Bigfoot was out and about. No Bigfoot, but she couldn't shake the feeling that there were eyes on her the whole run. Probably just some moose or something. She did her four miles, showered, had a cup of Folgers that wasn't as revolting as she anticipated, and headed for Roseburg since the tavern didn't serve breakfast and nowhere else around here did either.

RANDALL HAD SAID THE SECRETARY OF STATE OR THE attorney general had been interested in the thrashings of the Cultural Center. Perhaps somebody there could be of help. She called the Secretary of State's Office, got a lady who was in charge of overseeing nonprofit corporations, and learned that she should be talking to the deputy attorney general in charge of civil enforcement. Most enforcement is hardly civil, thought Lara, but maybe out here in uber-polite Orygun things were different.

After multiple transfers and annoying clicks on her heavy and by this time very hot mobile brick of a phone (Lara worried that the thing was frying her brain), she was connected with the Charitable Activities Section of the

Oregon Department of Justice. She didn't get the name of the person she was talking to and had trouble taking notes since she was sitting in her car, but she learned:

a. The Left Coast Cultural Center had been on their radar, initially for not registering with the state and getting the requisite license to do business. They had reluctantly complied.

b. There was an overlap between the Board of Trustees of the center and the board of Williams Lumber, one being a charitable organization (not for profit and charitable were the same in this case) and the other a taxable for-profit entity. Swapping funds was a no-no but the deputy attorney general, if that is what she was, could give no further information since the matter was "under ongoing investigation."

c. They had written several strong letters to the Cultural Center expressing concern, seeking cooperation for an audit, and threatening civil fines. Such replies as they had gotten were verbal and cursory.

d. A lawsuit for civil fines was possible.

e. The attorney general had contacted the IRS to investigate whether the actions or inactions of the Cultural Center were consistent with its tax-exempt status. The attorney general had said that charities are subsidized by the taxpayers and must operate in a way that justifies the public trust.

Lara asked if they had any operatives on the ground at Salish. The AG laughed and allowed as how her office didn't have any stormtroopers.

Orygun polite.

———————◆———————

I SHOULD HAVE ASKED HER WHO HER CONTACT PERSON WAS at the Cultural Center, thought Lara. But then, unless it was Mrs. Williams, that person probably isn't there anymore. And anyway, it looks as if the AG has kicked the investigation back to the IRS. She called Peter at the NEA's lawyer shop and filled him in on her talk with Oregon's lawyers. Peter had received no acknowledgement, let alone a response to his fax. Lara didn't have any problem with lawyers, she had even dated a few in the past, but they were, as a species, generally both patient and slow, and she was neither.

That is why, a half hour later, she was sitting in the office of Williams Lumber having requested an audience with the pope—with Bill Williams, himself. When asked by the secretary for the reason of her visit, she flashed her "light up the night" smile (the secretary was a guy) and said it was "personal."

I'll be damned if I will kiss his ring, she thought and then settled in to be ignored. But unlike his wife, he was not indisposed and asked her into his office and offered coffee. He was nice, polite, and careful.

She guessed him to be late fifties, lean and fit with hair greying at the temples, a quick smile, and bright blue eyes. A charmer.

"What can I do for you, Ms. Cole? Cole. Are you related to Rufus Cole, by any chance? He and I go way back in the timber business."

"No, I am not from around here," she said, but before she could go on, he threw out another friend-bomb.

"My secretary said your visit was personal, and I think you will find that there is no friendlier, no more personable place than around here. This is God's country—best place in the world to live. Have you visited Steamboat? It is up the river a ways and has some of the best fly fishing you have ever had. You fish, don't you?"

"No, I just came in to…"

"And if you like clamming," he interrupted, "the coast is about an hour away. Razor clams fried in butter. Can't beat it."

Lara could see where this was going. He would review hunting, golf, football, god knows what else, and gently usher her out without her asking a thing, so she raised her hand as if she were in class. He paused, just long enough.

"I am here about the Left Coast Cultural Center. The place is locked up, and your wife will not talk to me. I want you to do something about it."

Silence.

"I don't interfere in my wife's affairs; you should talk to her."

"I tried, and the butler told me she was indisposed. The last time I went to your house, no one answered the door. Is there a phone number that will reach her?"

"The number is unlisted for obvious reasons," he said. His manner was still mild, a hint of a smile on his lips.

"I am asking you to help me here. I have been sent by the federal government to review and report on the Cultural Center. It has received a lot of taxpayer money and has obligations that perhaps are not being met."

"They have all sorts of employees who run the place. Go out there and ask them."

"Are you saying that you don't know the director has been fired, most of the trustees quit, and the place is locked up?"

"I am telling you that I deal with timber, not art, and you are talking to the wrong guy. But it was nice to meet you, and I hope you will enjoy your stay here."

Thus ended the next lesson in Orygun polite.

———————•—•———————

SINCE SHE WAS NEAR THE HARDWARE STORE THAT FRANK Bolinger owned, she thought she might as well stop in and see if he could tell her anything else. The wrappings and crumbs of his lunch sandwich were on the same table next to the counter. He actually looked pleased to see her.

"The art lady. Nice to see you again. It's Lara isn't it?"

"Yes, Mr. Bolinger, nice to see you, too, and thank you for remembering me."

"It has only been a day, and I am not senile yet. What's up?"

"Unfortunately, not much. Your friend Mary told me what she knew and referred me to Piper Williams, as did you. Piper won't see me, so I talked to her husband who didn't tell me diddly-squat."

"You saw the pope? Brave lady. Did his goons throw you out the door?"

"Actually, he was polite, and I didn't see any goons, but he just gave me a lathery line of bullshit and eased me out the door."

"That'd be Bill all right. He is a slick one."

"So is there anyone else I could talk to?"

"If you could find Josh Bendix, the director Piper fired, he might know a lot, but I don't know where he went. He lived here in Roseburg, not Salish, and he gave up his apartment and took off right after he got canned."

"What apartment?"

"The Grand Apartments. It's a yellow brick building, an old one, over on Stephens and Cass, not all that far from where the other hardware store blew up."

⁕

THE APARTMENT HOUSE IN WHICH JOSH BENDIX HAD lived had no office but posted a number for a resident manager. She extracted her electronic brick and dialed the number. No answer; no message machine.

⁕

LARA HAD HEARD WHAT SHE THOUGHT WAS AN UNUSUAL number of sirens for a small town, and she hoped the place was not going to blow up again. It was only midday, and she had gotten exactly nowhere, so she decided just for the hell of it to go back to the Victorian mansion and ring the bell to see if Mrs. Williams was still indisposed.

She rang.

The butler did not appear.

The door stayed closed.

She waited. And waited.

She leaned on the bell for another thirty seconds, made a rude gesture to the closed door, and left with her temper on simmer.

⁕

SHE THOUGHT ABOUT GOING BACK TO THE CLEAN, PRE-sentable dive tavern where the mesmerizing singer guy had caused her a stomach tickle the previous night, but it was too early, and she spanked her mind for acting like a bewildered high school love puppy.

Out of options and ideas, she drove slowly back to Salish, being passed by still more emergency vehicles, sirens wailing and lights ablaze.

CHAPTER 4

Most advice is bad advice.

I t was midafternoon when she arrived back in Salish, an hour that was too early or too late to do anything worthwhile. Her room was depressing so she wandered over to the tavern. It was open but empty save for an old guy nursing a beer and the bartender, this time female and sporting a "Beth" name tag. Lara mounted a stool and ordered a Coke. She got a Pepsi, without apology.

Old guy, without looking up from the eyeless gaze he had fixed on his beer, said, "Lotta sirens."

After a pause of about five beats, the bartender said, "Yeh."

Lara waited to see whose turn it was next.

Thirty seconds, this time, and the old guy said, "Found an abandoned auto."

Bartender: "So?"

Old guy shrugged. As far as Lara could tell, he didn't drink the beer. Just looked at it. She decided it was her turn. "Do they always drive fast and use their sirens for an abandoned car?"

Nobody said anything. Lara drank some Pepsi. Tasted awful; she had never liked soft drinks and only drank them if she had to order something and it was too early for alcohol.

Overcome with the stimulating dialogue, Lara slapped a couple of bucks on the bar and left.

What to do next?

Why not try to find out what the sirens were about? So she climbed in her car and followed the parade, at a safe distance. When she reached the entrance of a Forest Service road, it was clear she was going no farther because a sheriff's car, lights flashing, was parked across it. She pulled off onto the shoulder, put on her flashers, got out, and walked up, showing her hands away from her body (she was, after all, a city girl who knew how to not get shot). She stopped well away from the deputy who was standing there, and smiled.

He nodded.

She waited, hoping he would confess. No such luck.

"What's going on?" she asked.

"Too soon to tell," he said. "You a reporter?"

"No, I have been hired to do a review of the Left Coast Cultural Center, but it is all locked up."

"Heard that," he said.

"That I was here?" she said.

"No, that the place was locked up. We were asked to send a patrol by there every now and then to make sure nobody was messing with it."

"Why all the commotion about an abandoned car?"

"It is what is and isn't in the car that is causing the fuss," he said.

"What does that mean?"

"I can't tell you any more than that. You probably oughta scoot. Sometimes a gawker will be looking at the flashing lights and drive right into your car or mine."

She took his advice and scooted.

By now it was no longer too early to drink, so she returned to the tavern. The place was abuzz. She got a Dead Guy Ale and listened in. The car, they were guessing, could be that of Linda McKenzie, the young woman Piper Williams had chosen to replace the fired Josh Bendix at the center. She had promptly disappeared. The information was spotty and probably unreliable, but apparently there was blood and no sign of Linda. They had searchers out looking.

Oops. Nothing polite about this scenario.

She went back to her room, pulled out the electronic brick (which she did not entirely trust), and dialed the number of Josh Bendix's apartment manager. Still no answer and no message machine. She didn't want to go back to the tavern to eat so she drove to Roseburg and had Chinese. This time she succumbed to the high school love-puppy impulse and drove to the clean, presentable dive, but the sexcaster guy wasn't there so she didn't stay. Her mind's mind started to beat her up, but she slapped it down.

Thus endeth another day of no progress on the job she was there to do. In the morning she would call Randall and ask if she should just come home. She dreamt of being chased, not an unfamiliar dream, but Bigfoot was a new addition.

THE FOLGERS THE NEXT MORNING WAS NO BETTER, NO worse. Awake enough to unplug the brick from its charger (it was still plenty hot), she dialed the apartment manager again to try to track down fired Cultural Center director Josh Bendix. Somebody answered. This is going to be a good day.

"Hi, my name is Lara Cole, and I am trying to get in touch with Josh Bendix who used to live in your apartments."

"Hold on...Muriel, it's about the apartments...Just a minute."

"Hello." Lara repeated her first spiel.

"We don't give out personal information. Are you doing a credit check?"

"No, I am a professional colleague, a museum director, and I am trying to reach Josh about some business." That was all true. "He is a friend." That wasn't.

"If you are a friend, you should have his contact information."

Never lie unnecessarily—a maxim Lara had just violated. "I had his number at the Cultural Center, but there is nobody there. The place is locked up. It is important that I find him right away; I would really appreciate your help."

"Well, I am not going to give you his forwarding address, but there is a phone number here, and I suppose there is no harm in giving that to you."

She did.

Lara called it and got the voice of an older lady who turned out to be Josh's mother. Josh wasn't up yet, but she said he should be, and she would go get him.

After hearing a bleary "Hello," Lara introduced herself as an NEA site visitor to the Left Coast Cultural Center and wondered if he, Josh, could fill her in on some details.

"Oh, boy, are there ever details. Hold on while I get a cup of coffee, and I will fill your ear."

Her ear was already burning from the brick, so she put it down until she heard his voice again.

"I'm back and glad to talk to you because I signed the advancement grant application, and I don't want my reputation to go into the toilet along with that of the center. What you have to understand from the get-go is that the Williamses, both the pope and Piper, consider it to be their personal plaything. We had a board of trustees—I will tell you more about them in a minute—and a staff, of which I was the head, but nothing happened there without a papal blessing. And Piper, as the under-pope, was the one who always delivered the news about what we were going to do or not do. It was a totally untenable situation, and I would have quit if she hadn't fired me first."

"How long ago did you leave?"

"About a month. I am recharging the batteries here before I look for another job. Obviously I am not going to get a letter of recommendation from Piper."

"Did you know the place was locked up tight? There isn't even a guard to come to the door."

"No, I didn't, but that is very bad. There is some extremely valuable art in there. I was responsible for purchasing much of it, and the place is in the woods with nothing near it. Really bad, really bad."

"What can you tell me about the trustees?"

"Send in the clowns. We have—had—a conference room with glass windows facing the lobby, and we are sitting around the conference table when one of them—we called him Old Fuzzy—came steaming through the lobby and right into the glass wall. BOOM. Bent his glasses, and for weeks there was the "Old Fuzzy memorial smudge" on the glass where his nose hit. Another lady, without a clue about

Robert's Rules, kept saying: "I want to make a move." She wanted to make a motion, but perhaps she had to go to the bathroom, too?

"Another trustee, and he was one of the good ones, a guy who runs a hardware store—and I got this second-hand because it was after I was fired—but he was fed up with Piper pontificating, especially since she was only the under-pope, and he got up and said, 'I am too old and too rich to sit through this,' and he quit on the spot. But most of the trustees don't know anything about running a cultural center, and they could care less. I would see them leafing through the materials we had sent out a week before the meeting that they clearly had not read, let alone studied. To most of them, the financials might as well have been written in Sanskrit. They were there because it is a small town, and it pays to be on the good side of the powers that be. And the Williamses have more horsepower than all the other officeholders and mucky-mucks around there put together."

"Why were you fired?"

"I was getting increasingly uncomfortable with a lot of things and was starting to ask Piper some questions she didn't want to answer. A couple of the artworks were taken down, and she said they were being restored but was vague about who was doing what. Valuable pieces. When the pieces were returned and rehung, some of them just didn't look right. I don't know; it was just a feeling I got. Then there were some accounting discrepancies. Our cash on hand on the books and in the bank didn't match. And several of the trustees were also on the board of Williams Lumber. Our conflict-of-interest policy was written into the bylaws but honored in the breach.

"Every time I approached her, and she was hard to get to because her 'butler' always answered the phone and no one, I mean no one, gets into her house. So the only time I could talk to her was when she was actually at the center, and then she was always flitting around being busy and didn't have time to talk."

"I thought the butler was a strange affectation for Roseburg," said Lara.

"Butler, my ass. A guy who grew up around there told me he played football with that guy in high school before he put on an English accent and a pair of shoes. Anyway, Piper just up and fired me one day; no reason given, and to tell the truth, I was relieved. You have got your work cut out for you, Lara. The place is a mess."

"What about after you left?" asked Lara, "I am told that Linda McKenzie took over."

"Linda is a nice young woman. I hired her, but don't confuse gregarious with competent. She is fresh out of school and in no way prepared to handle an institution with as much going on as the Cultural Center. She is good with computers, and we were in the process of going totally electronic, so that was what she was supposed to do. Not a chance she could withstand Piper. Piper will have her for lunch."

"She has apparently disappeared. Do you know how to get ahold of her?" asked Lara.

"She's gone, too? Bad news. She has some Oregon roots; Medford, I think, and her father was connected to the college in Ashland—music, maybe?"

CHAPTER 5

There is no cure for curiosity.

R andall at the NEA had told Lara to hang around for a few more days; this after she had related all that she had discovered to date (which was more about what she hadn't found out). His view was that if there were irregularities in the way their grantee was using federal money, they couldn't just let it slide. He would contact the IRS and see if they could add some enforcement muscle. He wasn't optimistic. His words, although Lara didn't capture them exactly, were something like "the rest of the government is more interested in dollars and missiles than paintings and sculpture."

The town (barely) of Salish had expended its meager supply of charm so Lara decided to move to Roseburg where she could find a regular motel, a restaurant, and perhaps some more information. And that singer guy was tumbling around in her brain in a most disconcerting way. Her move completed, she put on her running gear and set out for a cruise around the city. This was her routine whenever she traveled—either run or walk the town—you can't really get the feel of a place from a car. Sure, she had gotten into some sketchy neighborhoods, but she figured she could outrun any pursuers. That, plus she knew a little karate. She wasn't careless of her own safety, or ignorantly brave, but she persisted in the notion that her life was happening to someone else. And anyway, wasn't it Aldo Leopold who said it is a poor life that achieves freedom from fear?

Her other habit in getting to know a place was to snag a local paper and read the letters to the editor. There was lots to learn, particularly about a small town, by reading what the locals care about, and unlike big cities, the language was often unpolished, unapologetic, and hilarious. That is where she found the story about a casket that had turned up in the local cemetery. It was apparently dumped there, above ground, not buried, but locked, and it didn't have a note pinned to it like the sweater of a kindergartner. It also didn't bear a mortuary identifying number, and nobody knew where it had come from or whom it contained. The letter writer wondered if the city officials were so damned busy that they couldn't track down the dear departed. Caskets weren't furniture, she wrote, put the damn thing in the ground and have some respect, for heaven's sake.

Not something you read about every day, thought Lara, and having nothing better to do, she dropped in to the newspaper office to chat up the editor. Here central casting had done its job. He was sixties, two-day stubble, sleeves rolled up, no tie, and a sign on his desk that said "Thank you for not asking me not to smoke." He was off with his questions before she sat down, voice coming through his nose; little puffs of smoke coming out with each word. Who was she, why was she here, what had she found out, was it the National Endowment for the Arts that funded the sculpture commemorating the Big Blast? Lara answered and eventually the exchange morphed into a smoke infested conversation rather than an interrogation.

Lara: "So what can you tell me about Mr. and Mrs. Bill Williams?"

Editor: "He is the big lumber guy around here and she, the arts maven."

Lara: "And…"

Editor: "And, he owns this paper. Next topic."

Lara: "What can you tell me about the Left Coast Cultural Center?"

Editor: "It has been a real cultural tourism draw. It has a fine collection of Native American Art, and some early works of Northwest artists who have made the big time. There is a lot of what we call 'rural wisdom' that shows up in some of the best local artists, and when they get discovered by the 'urban folks'—the galleries in New York and LA—we can't afford to collect them anymore. And then we have a bunch of Soviet stuff, most of which I find totally depressing."

Lara: "You say 'we.'"

Editor: "A proprietary pride of local ownership. I don't have anything to do with the Cultural Center except to write about their shows and bang the drum…sorry, not trying to be disrespectful to our Native culture…be a cheerleader for the local area."

Lara: "Do you know why it is locked up?"

Editor: "Can't help you there."

Lara: "Can't or won't?"

Editor: Shrugs. Lights new cigarette from the smoked one.

Lara: "What's the story on the coffin that got dumped in the cemetery?"

Editor: "I don't want you to think we get two or three of those a week. I've never had a story like that as long as I have been here. It is a young lady in the box, but she hasn't been identified yet. Foul play almost certainly. I can't write about it until the authorities cough up some info and they aren't saying much so far."

Lara: "Who is she?"

Editor: "Don't know."

Lara: "Big trouble."

She got up and hurried out.

———————⋆⋅◆⋅⋆———————

Nothing to do is sometimes the hardest job in the world. A multitude of thoughts were knocking about in the uncharted backwaters of Lara's brain, not the least of which was why hadn't the authorities identified the poor woman in the casket? With equal measures of ignorance and confidence, she set about using the feet in her shoes.

First stop was the police station, where no one was prepared to tell her anything. Next, she called the state police. Same response.

Surely they could take the dead lady's fingerprints, but unless she had been in the military, afoul of the law, or in a job that required a security clearance, she would not show up.

She wondered how to find out if there were reports of a missing person. Wouldn't the police look at those?

She sucked it up and made the call she least wanted to make: to Southern Oregon College (soon to be university, its promotional material said) in Ashland where she asked to be connected to a staff member named McKenzie—music she thought.

"Jack McKenzie," he answered.

"Professor McKenzie, my name is Lara Cole. I am out here doing a review of the Left Coast Cultural Center, and

I would like to talk to the acting director, who I think may be related to you."

"That would be my daughter, Linda, but I don't understand why you are calling me."

"When did you last talk to her?"

"She called…probably ten days ago. Are you in Roseburg? Why don't you go to the center and talk to her?"

"The center is locked up, and there is nobody around."

"What? Now you've got me concerned. She hasn't told us anything like that. Are you sure?"

"Yes, perhaps you could call her."

"Hold on, I will try her on another line. If I lose you, please call back," he said and gave his direct dial number.

Lara put down the brick—a real hot potato that was probably hoovering up her brain cells by the minute.

He came back on the line. "She doesn't answer, either at the center or where she lives."

"I don't want to alarm you, professor, but it might be a good idea to try to track her down through her friends or coworkers or whatever, and if you find her, I would appreciate a call." She gave him the number of the brick.

This is really ugly and likely to get a lot worse. She hoped she was wrong.

———◆——

WHAT ABOUT THE CAR THAT THEY FOUND IN THE WOODS? It had to be registered to somebody. The local police couldn't be that dumb. And if someone had kidnapped Linda, wouldn't there be a ransom demand? And if she was the one in the casket, why would the killer make such a public display? What message was being conveyed?

She had one more resource, but she was afraid she was getting ahead of herself. She had a habit of sticking in when it was none of her business, but, she thought, that is just the way I am, so screw it.

She called George Graham at the FBI.

Not everyone has her own special FBI agent, but George Graham and Lara had thoroughly bonded in a shootout in Russia. It was that damn icon thing that seemed to follow her around like a noxious odor. She looked on Graham as a father—loved him like the father she never had.

Graham had filed multiple discrimination complaints in his climb through the ranks of the FBI and was now a top agent, widely respected, and mentor to junior agents of all races. Black, bald, and now thick, not fat, he adored Lara and was thrilled to hear from her.

"Sweet Pea!"

"Hello George. How goes the never-ending fight against crime and corruption?"

"A losing battle. Are you in DC? I will buy you lunch if you don't mind going to a food cart."

"Such a temptation, but no, I am in Roseburg, Oregon, and if you have a minute, I would like to run something by you."

"Where is Roseburg. For that matter, where is Oregon?"

"The locals pronounce it Orygun, and you can't be serious. I am going to assume you aren't, so here is what is happening. I am out here to do a site visit, essentially an investigation, of a cultural center—kind of a museum—that has received a big grant from the National Endowment for the Arts. The place is locked up, no one will talk to me, the former director has been fired, and the acting director is missing and maybe dead. The NEA chair has alerted the IRS to investigate, but nothing to my knowledge is happening there, so what would you suggest I do?"

"Lara, you do know how to find trouble. My advice is to get the hell out of there, and go back to your own museum."

"Don't you guys have jurisdiction over kidnappings?"

"Children and those taken over state lines. Sometimes the locals ask for help, but we can't just bust in there 'cause you are the suspicious type."

"Well, could you call the locals and see what is up? They have a body of a young female who might be the acting director, and they can't seem to find their ass with both hands."

"My, you do have a way with words. Sweetie, I can't do that as much as I love you. Just cool your jets, and let things take their course. Will you do that for me, please? I fear for your safety if you get in the middle of whatever is going on, and I don't want to have to try to save you and get shot again."

She whined some more, but he wouldn't budge, so she sent kisses and hung up.

CHAPTER 6

Ethics is about action in the face of uncertainty.

L inda McKenzie was dead.

Murdered.

She was the lady in the casket. It was all over the morning paper.

Lara didn't know if George Graham had stirred the pot, or if Linda's father had made the connection, or if the locals had figured it out, but there it was. The car they had found with blood in it was a rental. The renter was the Cultural Center. Dead end.

"What am I doing here?" Introspection kept bothering her, which is why, when it showed up, she turned off that switch. She put the feeling on the stage in her mind and closed the curtain. Her cognitive escape—except it wasn't working. Why was she here? Why didn't she tell Randall that this site visit was a bust and catch the next plane home? What notches would she put on her revolver handle if she did something brave? (She didn't have a revolver. It was just a stupid western metaphor.) Maybe she wouldn't mind being dead? Was that it? Had she, at age 35, exhausted life's mystery? Was art just another commodity in commerce that was fungible and valuable only in shekels? Was she, as she feared, doing a mind-douche on herself?

Lara's lover, Michael Solak, had been shot and killed in Moscow trying to protect a priceless Eastern Orthodox icon. Lara's memory of that tragedy was glued to her neural pathways, as post-traumatic stress is wont to do. When his life ended so did part of hers. But on the positive side of the ledger, she felt his presence as a brilliant force within her—a motivating and calming energy—a determination to live two lives as one and to welcome each day she could do so. His soul had migrated into her body. Aristotle would approve.

She had tools to get rid of the black dog in her mind. She knew how to embrace the positive, so she put on her running gear and started out at a brisk pace to rearrange the serotonin in her brain—those wiggly vipers that devoured her confidence. It worked well enough and after a shower she felt better, but still was unsure what she was doing here.

Yes, Linda McKenzie was dead, but what concern was that of hers? And if it were her concern—beyond that for all living things—the smallest sparrow falling from the sky and all that— what could she do about it? She stood in front of the bathroom mirror and gave herself "the talk": You are worthy because you are you. You are part of a living organism that is the earth. You are responsible to yourself first and to all others second.

Her shoulders sagged; her hair looked stringy. She felt small and pale and defeated. She screamed at the mirror: "Stay positive!" and hated the way her mouth looked while forming the words. Her self-confidence was in the dumpster, and she didn't even know why. This wasn't another failure in the great scorecard in the sky; she just couldn't do the job she had come to do. And it wasn't her fault. She felt as if she needed another run. The phone rang instead.

"Is this Lara Cole?" It was. "This is Juan Oropallo. I am an investigator with the Oregon Department of Justice. We have been looking into the affairs of the Left Coast Cultural Center since they are a nonprofit and don't seem to have much regard for the laws they are supposed to obey."

"You are, Mr. Oropallo, a breath of fresh air. I have been trying to find an ally out here for days, and frankly nobody seems to give a shit."

"Aside from being called fresh air, which I suppose is a compliment, kind of, I would be happy to sit down and compare notes, since, I am told, you are here to check up on the place, too."

Coffee in a half hour at the local Starbucks.

OROPALLO WAS ROUND AND HAPPY. DARK HAIR, STOCKY body, big smile, about Lara's age. He was the kind of disarming person you just wanted to talk to. They told each other what they knew about the Cultural Center. It was a conversation with a lot of questions and very few answers.

"The attorney general is the state's top cop. Can't you just get some heavies in here, and we will open the center—break in if we have to—and then we can both do our jobs."

"There must be somebody we can find who has a key."

"I have tried Mrs. Piper Williams, and she won't even see me."

"Let me call the general and ask her to make the request. I can't imagine Piper Williams refusing to talk to the attorney general."

But that is exactly what happened. Then the governor called the attorney general and told her to back off. Then the general called Oropallo and told him to back off. Did the Williamses have the juice? Better believe it.

"So what do you do now, Juan?" asked Lara. "Just go back and lick your wounds?"

"All this tells me is that there is a lot to be found if we can ever get at the books and stuff. That means I will stick around and act like a professional investigator who only temporarily has his thumb up his ass."

"Good plan," said Lara, "and I will make a few calls on this exciting new portable phone" holding it up for him to see.

"I hear those fry your brain."

———————◆•———————

She called George Graham at the FBI again. He was both pleased and unhappy to hear from her.

"Sweetie, I hope you are calling me from your home in the Blue Ridge with that grey cat on your lap."

"Ah, no, I am still here in Oregon, but you should know a couple more things. The state attorney general tried to get her investigator into the Cultural Center, and the governor ordered her to back off, obviously at the behest of the Williamses, who are the local power brokers and the wife of whom is the head of the center's trustees. The AG has already asked the IRS to intervene, so I am wondering if you could shake a few trees and maybe get the IRS to send somebody out here who has enough authority to get the place open."

"You are telling me the governor doesn't want you in there?"

"I think it is more accurate to say that the governor doesn't want to piss off the Williamses."

"Smells kinda stinky. My better judgment has caught the morning train where you are concerned, Lara. I will see what I can do."

Two hours later he called back. "The United States attorney for the district of Oregon is going to seek an order from the federal court to gain access for the IRS and you, and, I suppose the state AG, to the culture place. All this means is you can get in. It doesn't, assuming the judge grants the order, mean that you have carte blanche to do anything you want. Be careful, Lara. It seems to me the stakes here are higher than just a little review of the books."

WHAT HAPPENED NEXT WAS THAT THE US ATTORNEY FOR the district of Oregon appeared before Judge Leighton Carver in Eugene with a Petition for Entry and Examination in a case titled "*United States of America v. Left Coast Cultural Center.*" The petition stated that the Department of Revenue (IRS) and the National Endowment for the Arts both had standing to review the affairs of the Cultural Center and had been unable to gain access despite multiple efforts. Taxpayer money was at issue, and the case clearly fell within the case or controversy jurisdiction of the federal court.

Judge Carver had questions for the lawyer who appeared on behalf of the center. Mainly he wanted to know what the hell was going on and why the place was locked up and nobody was cooperating. He tolerated a few evasive answers, cut the lawyer off, and issued an order that the federal marshals would provide access, either by obtaining a key or breaking down the door. So there.

THE US MARSHALS SERVICE IS ONE OF THE LESSER known but quietly effective branches of law enforcement. They carry sidearms and are empowered to keep the peace and promote the swift efficiency of the justice system. They showed up the next day and knocked on the big oaken door of Piper Williams's Victorian mansion. The butler responded, gave the faux-English response that he would see if Mrs. Williams was available, started to close the door, and found it smartly pushed back in his face. It is axiomatic that federal marshals take no shit. In plain English they informed him that Mrs. Williams would present herself with the key right now, or they would tear the place apart until they found it.

The butler returned—Mrs. Williams, poised and imperious, in his wake.

"Gentlemen, what can I do for you?"

"This is a petition and order of access, madam. Please provide us with a key to the Cultural Center. It would be a good idea to have some guards there as well since the place will be unlocked."

"Oh, dear, this is very confusing. I will have to have my lawyer look this over before I can agree."

"You don't have the option of agreeing or not, and your lawyer has already appeared and argued before the judge. So please give us the key. Now. Your failure to do so would be an obstruction of justice and might land you in jail."

"My, you gentlemen are determined. I don't, however, react well to threats."

"Lady, we're not here to be polite. Unless you want to be handcuffed and your house searched, we will have the key, and we mean now."

They got it, along with a promise from Mrs. Williams that they would be hearing from her lawyer, which stuck them as pretty funny since they had already seen the judge dismantle him.

———————◆————◆————

LARA HAD MOVED BACK TO THE SUITES IN SALISH— honest to god, that's what he called them—since she thought she could get her work done in a couple of days and be out of there. She was tired of driving back and forth to Roseburg. On the way, she identified the spot the locals called "goat hill." It was local lore, she was told, that you could predict the weather by the level at which the goats were grazing. It was a medium-high goats day. Fair weather.

The federal marshals, whose names were Bradley and Lester, had Mrs. Williams's key, and it opened the front door. Unfortunately, that is all it did. The art of the permanent collection that was on display was accessible, and that of the special show of contemporary Northwest art, but the administrative offices where the financial records were kept were locked, and the single key they had obtained didn't open them.

Lara huddled with Juan Oropallo, Lester, and Bradley. The marshals were used to miscreants who didn't want to cooperate, usually because they were guilty and had a lot to hide. It was all in a day's work for them, so they drove back to the Victorian mansion and pounded on the door. It was early, just after 8 a.m. and who should come to the door in his bathrobe but Bill Williams. The pope. He was not pleased to see them.

He told them:

a. It was awfully early. Please come back at a reasonable hour.
b. He didn't know a thing about the doings of the Cultural Center.
c. They needed to understand that his wife didn't work there; she was a volunteer doing her charitable duty.
d. The "strong-arm" tactics they had visited on her the previous day had traumatized her, and she would not be available for an extended period.
e. He would be in touch with Oregon's US senators (he called them Fred and Andy) to get to the bottom of this intrusion.

He was perfectly polite during all of this. He didn't raise his voice and spoke with the kind of quiet condescension that a multimillionaire and self-anointed pope would apply to scruffy vassals.

Bradley and Lester, having worked together for years, by silent communication, declined to throw the pope to the ground, robe flying, put a knee in his back, and cuff him. They bid Williams good day and went to call the US attorney in Portland. Up the chain it went. The US attorney called the attorney general of the United States. The attorney general called the head of the FBI and the chairman of the

National Endowment for the Arts (first such call he had ever received from the attorney general, and it scared the pants off him). The question was, beyond what was going on, why was this becoming, literally and figuratively, a federal case? Nobody knew.

Then staffers from both Oregon US senators called to ask the same questions. They made it clear that their bosses were "interested" and that congressional oversight for an important constituent would be exercised. They didn't mention that both Williams and Williams Lumber were big-time contributors to their bosses' continued presence in Washington.

MEANTIME, LARA AND JUAN OROPALLO WALKED AROUND the Cultural Center, taking inventory of the place. It was palatial. The galleries were state of the art with quiet but efficient lighting, all of the necessary climate controls, wide aisles, and comfortable benches for contemplation of some very respectable art. Security was off, which was puzzling. With no guards in the building, and no alarms set, the place was a sitting duck, that is if there were any art hunters in this neck of the woods. Probably more hunters of actual ducks. But still, this was way beyond unprofessional with a valuable collection supported by a bunch of government money. There were a couple of spots on the walls where art clearly had been, but they had no way of knowing why the pieces were not currently where the labels on the wall said they should be.

George Graham had called Lara to tell her that she had really stirred up a hornet's nest. He didn't tell her to back off; just to be careful. He warned that with the number of fingers in the pie, things were likely to go very slowly and that they might have to go back to the judge to be sure their next moves had his approval. Randall at the NEA called and was clearly out of his depth: giddy on the one hand that the NEA was finally getting some attention from the other parts of the government, and scared shitless on the other that he would be dragged into a battle in which he had no troops and precious few weapons. He signed off telling Lara he was counting on her.

To do what?

Then the thugs from Williams Lumber arrived.

CHAPTER 7

Art speaks its own language.

They arrived in a dusty and dented pickup. Their pants were uncuffed and hung at the tops of their boots. They reached back in the truck to get their hard hats, pushed them onto their heads, looked at the two marshals standing near the door, walked up to Lara and Juan and announced: "We're here to protect the statues."

One was big and brawny and hooked his thumbs in his suspenders as he spoke. The man with him was shorter, stockier, dressed the same, and spat a chaw while his partner declared their mission. Traditional museum guards, they were not.

Lara: "Who sent you?"

Logger I (the tall one): "The boss said we was to come up here and make sure you people who have the key don't make off with any of the stuff."

Lara: "How are you going to do that?"

Logger II (the stocky one): "We are going to watch you, and if you try to take stuff we will take it back and beat the crap out of you in the process."

Logger I: "And we will be relieved by some of our friends, so we will be here 24/7 in case you try to get tricky and steal stuff at night."

Lara: "The two gentlemen here in the blue blazers and grey slacks are US marshals. I tell you that just so you won't make any mistake about who you are dealing with."

Logger II (clearly the more aggressive): "We have plenty of friends who won't stand still for the feds comin' in here and screwin' with us. Those dudes may have pea shooters under them jackets, but our friends and us can blow anybody who stands in our way to kingdom come, and we are locked and loaded."

Through this prickly exchange, Lester and Bradley stood relaxed and amused, but Lara noticed that they had unbuttoned their jackets.

"Hey, Josh, how would you like to work for the NEA?" Lara was on the electronic brick to the former head of the Left Coast Cultural Center, Josh Bendix.

"Doing what?"

"We have finally gotten into the Cultural Center, but we can't get into the offices where the records are. Since there isn't anyone here to guide us, it would be really helpful if you could come up and show us where the bodies are buried."

"Not funny, Lara. I heard about Linda McKenzie."

"Sorry, Josh, I wasn't trying to be cute. I have talked to Randall, and he is willing to pay you an hourly rate plus expenses out of the chairman's discretionary fund. All you would have to do is answer questions and show us where things are."

"Is this likely to be dangerous, Lara? I am a confirmed coward when it comes to rough stuff, and my will to stay alive is enormous."

"There are federal marshals here, and they are armed. It should only take a couple of days, and then you can go back to sleeping late. By the way, you wouldn't have a key to the offices, would you?"

"I turned in all my stuff when I was canned. Piper Williams was right there with her hand palm up and her clipboard of stuff I should deliver." Dramatic pause. "But…but there is a hidden key to the offices. We stashed it because a number of us who worked there kept locking ourselves out, and it was a pain to have to get a guard to let us in every time."

"Bless you, Josh. How soon can you be here? Oh, and when you come, wear a blue blazer, grey slacks, and a dull tie. I'll tell you why when you arrive."

* * *

Logging has always been dangerous. Some of the danger is unavoidable. A tree can shatter, a cable break, brakes on a steep grade can fail. A radio signaling device called a Talkie-Tooter has a mercury switch and if it malfunctions, or the operator uses it wrong, the yarder may start reeling in the line unexpectedly. A logger who gets caught in the bite of the line has a very short life expectancy.

Some of the danger is invited, like the high climber who tops a 200-foot tree for a spar pole and then does a dance on top of the swaying trunk. The traditional logger is a tough dude; comfortable in the woods, accustomed to hard physical labor—and unlikely to take much guff from "city folk."

The logging business was changing fast in the last decade of the 20th century. In the late 1940s an Oregon guy named Cox was eating his lunch when he noticed a bark beetle larva, a worm about the size of a finger, eating through both rotted and fresh wood with its overlapping, opposing jaws. Cox figured if he could replicate those jaws in metal, he would be on to something. He did, and he was. His Cox Chipper Chain company became Omark Industries, and within a couple of decades it had cornered about 80 percent of the world's saw chain market.

While chainsaws replaced axes and hand saws (the old two-man "misery whip"), logging was turning toward hydraulics, electronics, and tracked and rubber-tired vehicles to do what men on the ground had traditionally done. The "Blue Ox" skidder was invented in the early 1960s to be followed by machines that could grab a tree, whack off the limbs, cut it into sections, and do most everything but take it to the mill. Computers were the big new thing, promising to make logging even more complex, more efficient, and more technical.

Where did this leave the traditional cork-booted loggers? It was a scary time for them. Not only were they being left behind by the technical revolution, but the goddamned environmentalists cared more about the goddamned spotted owl than their ability to feed their goddamned families. And every time it looked like a new side (section of the forest) would open up and provide some work, the goddamned owl huggers and the goddamned politicians and the goddamned local elected weenies would start gassing at each other, and then there would be thirty goddamned lawsuits in the goddamned courts where some senile goddamned judge would fart around on the case for a couple of goddamned years.

Goddammit.

Loggers were still tough, and now they were tough and frustrated and afraid—a volatile mixture.

In the board room of Williams Lumber seven guys sat around the table. All but two were smoking. Cigarettes, not cigars, and not, heaven forbid, pipes. Most of these were businessmen, and they maybe had a suit or two and a sport coat in the closet. But their everyday garb was off the rack at the Grange Co-op, and the pickups they drove were made in the you-ess-of-ay. The subject of the day was whether to further automate the Roseburg mill. They had the optical scanners, and the computers to maximize salable product from each log, but they needed to figure out if there was money to be made from pulping the small diameter trees they had traditionally left standing. Gone were the days when they just burned up crap wood in wigwam burners. The environmental agencies were all over them like smelly sweat socks to reduce smoke and pollution. Most of them thought that was a good idea—as long as it didn't cost too much.

Bill Williams ran the meeting. His style was quiet and informal. He deferred to the opinions of his board members, particularly to the one who was still actually working in the woods as a logger. The idea was to make the working grunts feel as if they had a say in what went on. Williams was unfailingly polite and, in the end, did exactly as he pleased. It was his company.

That was all right with the logger-board member, as long as he could keep doing what he was doing.

———————◆——

JOSH BENDIX HAD AGREED TO DRIVE UP FROM SAN FRAN-
cisco to his old museum, but Lara advised him not to go
directly there. She didn't want him to arrive unprepared,
and she didn't want the cork-booted guards to see his
car. He knocked on the door of her "suite" in Salish. He
was wearing a blue blazer, slacks that looked kind of grey,
although that may not have been their original color, and a
whitish shirt, tie knotted loosely at the neck. Perfect.

"You must be Lara. I see you are living in style. Have
you been to the tavern next door? Oldest continuous booze
joint in the West."

"The accommodations are the finest Salish has to offer,
and the reputation of the tavern gets grander at every repeti-
tion. Come in here," she said, grabbing his hand and pulling
him into the room.

She motioned to the single chair and sat on the bed
facing him. "First, thank you for coming. Where did you
park your car?"

"On the gravel to the side of the building next to the
pickups there."

"Good. While you are here I want you to ride with me.
It is just as well if they don't know what you are driving."

"Whoa. This is getting off to a scary start. You told
me there was no danger, and I told you what a chicken I
was...am."

"Since I talked to you some loggers showed up saying
they were there to guard the place. There are also federal
marshals there who are armed and have been dispatched

to enforce the court's order giving us access. I asked you to wear the blazer and slacks so they will think you are part of the Marshals Service. You will be with me and appear as if you are my bodyguard. Everything should be cool."

"I'm telling you right now, Lara, that if any rough stuff starts, I expect *you* to protect me."

"No problem."

She then went over the day's work, telling him about Juan Oropallo, the state attorney general's investigator who was on their side, and the two marshals, Lester and Bradley, with whom he should schmooze occasionally to show that they were colleagues.

"You know the most about what we should be looking at, so please guide us, but be subtle, remembering you are a marshal, not a museum guy. When you retrieve the hidden key to the offices, be sure the loggers don't see where it is kept. And don't take off your blazer. I don't want them to know you aren't packin'."

"I think I will get back in my car and drive the hell back to San Francisco as fast as I can."

She grabbed his sleeve and jerked him back into his chair. "Josh, where is your sense of adventure? Look on this as a caper you can embellish for your grandchildren."

"If I do this caper, I may not have any grandchildren."

She took him to the tavern for lunch and a beer to get up his courage.

WHEN LARA AND JOSH ARRIVED AT THE CULTURAL Center, the loggers, sitting and smoking at the end of the parking lot in chairs they had retrieved from the building, paid them scant attention. Good so far. Josh retrieved the key and let them into the offices, then replaced it so they all would have access, should he not be around. He was already getting morbid.

The next order of business was to do a quick tour. Josh pointed out the places where artworks were missing. They were two of the finest and most valuable of the collection. Piper had been vague about why they were taken down, but if her explanation that they were being restored was true, they should have been back by now. This further upset him, as if two of his children had been kidnapped. He kept muttering about where they had gone. He said lots of the pieces that were still there looked or felt different. He couldn't explain it.

In the office, the most notable feature was that all of the computers were gone. By this time, Josh was pale and trembling, and it was all Lara could do to keep him from passing out. She sat him down and told him to put his head between his knees and breathe into his cupped hands. She gave him water and stroked his neck, and after a while, he straightened up, shook his head, gave a wry smile, and said he was okay.

Meanwhile, Juan had been poking about and had come up with some files that looked promising. One appeared to hold printouts of balance sheets, another looked like profit and loss statements. They took these to the conference table for examination. Lara asked where the Memorial Nose Smudge was on the glass wall. A little levity. The glass wall was helpful to know if the logger-guards were nosing about.

The records didn't mean much to Lara, or Juan, but Josh was fascinated.

"Anybody who is fascinated by a balance sheet is far too easily entertained," said Lara.

"No, this is remarkable," replied Josh. "Usually we are scrounging for money, but the cash balance shown here is amazing. It says we have $497,567, and I have no idea where that could have come from."

"Well, some of it would be NEA money," Lara said.

"Maybe, but that shouldn't be in unrestricted cash. It could be sloppy bookkeeping, I suppose. The NEA distribution was $125,000, so there is a lot more here that came from somewhere else."

"A donation, perhaps?" asked Juan.

"It would have to have been a big one, and this statement is from while I was still here, and I surely would have known of such a gift," said Josh.

For the rest of the afternoon they went through the papers in the office. There was lots of paper, but the most recent stuff had been done on the computers that were no longer there. Josh told them that the now dead Linda McKenzie had been hired in part because, being younger and more electronically savvy, she could oversee the center's transition away from paper recordkeeping.

At the end of the afternoon, they left all the documents in place, put the files back where they had found them, locked up the offices, and prepared to run the gauntlet past the loggers.

"Are they going to try to search us?" asked Josh.

"They can try to search me," said Lara, "and I will submit with a smile, but if they touch the wrong places, they will get kneed in the balls. Josh, you stand clear. I don't think they will bother you, but if they do, call over the real marshals, who will tell them that federal agents don't get searched by loggers."

CHAPTER 8

An adult, by definition, has full moral agency.

———◆———

Piper Marsh Williams hadn't always been rich, nor had she been tutored in how to be rich. She was, however, a good student with a good mind and a fierce will to have the world on her own terms. She had grown up in Drain, a little Oregon town in the boonies, with a name only slightly more alluring than another Oregon town named Boring. What kids who grew up in Drain instinctively knew was that if you didn't want to go down, you had to get out.

She, Piper Marsh, went to community college in Sutherlin, a small town just north of Roseburg, and started looking around for opportunity. Taking stock of her assets, she knew that she wasn't pretty, but she was handsome: tall with good posture and strong facial features. She also was sexy, and she didn't mind sending off signals. She was good at that.

Williams Lumber was the biggest employer around, and the Williams family was the local royalty. Williams senior, locally known as the pope (church and state separation did not exist here), presided over most everything that went on, from local parades to high school football to deciding who got to be mayor (a largely ceremonial position since the pope called the shots).

Mrs. Pope—that is, Mrs. Williams—played a subservient and often invisible role. She hosted a few parties, so Piper had heard, bore a few children, and seemed to walk several steps behind her husband. So if you got to choose, thought Piper, would you rather be the pope or the wife? She couldn't be the pope without a gender transplant, but she could be the power behind the scepter if she observed as much as she could of what the current Mrs. Williams did, and then did the opposite.

The first order of business was to check out the rest of the Williams family to find out if any of them were fuckable. Senior Williams probably was, but what good would that do her? There were two Williams boys and one daughter. Bill, or Billy or Junior, was the oldest and the heir apparent to the popedom, but he was away at Harvard and not within seducible range, at least not during the school year. He was, however, potentially horny, since Harvard's student body was, at that time, gender singular—all male.

Second in line was Melissa, called Missy, and while Piper had no hang-ups about getting it on in a gender-inclusive fashion, femaleness was not going to get her where she wanted to go, not in the lumber-heavy, testosterone-driven financial world of Roseburgery.

That left the youngest Williams kid, Bertrand, called Bertie. And Bertie just happened to be sitting across the aisle from her in an accounting class at the community college. He was not getting it. He couldn't get straight which side of the balance sheet debits and credits were supposed to be on. He wasn't too good at math, and he didn't seem to appreciate that the whole idea behind a balance sheet was that things should, you know, balance.

This stuff came pretty naturally to Piper. Like sports ability or being able to match a pitch and sing, Piper understood math. For that matter, she understood money and how it worked and multiplied, even if she didn't have any. She would get it; money, that is. Of that she was certain. So she befriended Bertie and was patient with him and over numerous cups of coffee, explained accounting to his bewildered countenance while she judiciously pumped him about his family's affairs (their interactions, not their trysts). From this she learned when Billy would be back in town, what he liked to do (softball, beer, fast cars), whether he had a girlfriend (there was a chick he had had the hots for in high school, and she was still around), and if Billy would join the family business upon graduation (absolutely).

Piper then set about eliminating the competition by slandering the reputation of the high school chick Billy had the hots for. She fed Bertie all manner of salacious falsehoods about the poor chick with full confidence that this information would get to Billy's scrotum like a social disease. Then, when Billy came within fuckable distance, it was game on.

They became an item. She seduced him six ways from Sunday, and, somewhat to her surprise, she came to like him. He, on the other hand, was so thoroughly captured that he would do whatever she asked of him. She became Piper Williams, and Piper Marsh was history. She was the power behind the throne before he had a throne. Then Bill senior had a fortuitous fatal heart attack, and Piper was able to move the heartbroken and compliant Mrs. Williams senior out of the Victorian mansion to more suitable quarters for the former sub-pope. Wahoo.

The Left Coast Cultural Center was Piper's idea. She knew that sophisticated ladies liked art, or pretended to. She knew that culture attracted other culture and that if she was to hobnob with the rich and famous, she needed a home base. She knew that Bill would fork over the money to get the place going, and that with all the fancy wood in it, it would be a showplace for his products. It needed to be filled with stuff, preferably of some quality, and for that she could hire fancy "art advisors" who could help her find the best stuff that was out there—even some stuff of questionable provenance (she had learned the lingo of the art trade) and some that was probably stolen, but who was really going to check. She even liked some of the pictures.

One of the art advisors who had been particularly helpful, both while and after putting the Cultural Center together, was a Russian named Sergei Ashkenazy, maybe a Jew, who went by the first name Sam. She needed Sam now and called him.

<hr />

Lara had run the 400-meter in college. It is a sprint, not a run, once around the track as fast as you can go; a killer of a race because it requires both speed and stamina, and, if you are a star, a turbocharged extra gear at the finish. Lara was good, not great. She won some meets but had no illusions of Olympic grandeur. But she was a lifelong athlete and appreciated the benefits of staying in shape, which is why she had set off at first light from the "suites" in Salish and was running up a Forest Service road. She held to her default pace, and after about the first two minutes where the body rebels and the heart rate has not yet come awake, she was cruising, feeling as if she could go forever. She loved that sensation—the runner's high—an adrenal rapture.

She heard a small engine start somewhere behind her. They get to work early out here in the forest, she thought. She kept on running, up small rises and around corners with thick stands of trees on either side and a gentle upward grade. This was the life, with low humidity and crisp morning air. Maybe she should move from the humid and crowded East. She could probably find a job out here. She let her mind roll on. More engine noise from behind. She was coming to another bend and glanced over her shoulder to see a guy on a four-wheeler coming up behind her, and as she got around the corner, there was a pickup across the road with a guy standing by the tailgate.

Trouble.

To turn around was to go back to the four-wheeler, and she surely could not outrun it. So she kicked it into gear, maybe not a turbo, but good enough, jumped one foot on the pickup fender and the other on the hood (CRUNCH) and leapt off the other side like a steeple-chaser. The road was now climbing more steeply, and she could hear engines revving behind her. As soon as the pickup was out of the way, the four-wheeler would be on her like flies on cow flop.

Not many choices.

She swerved off to her right and into the trees, dodging and weaving between the ponderosa and lodgepole pines, leaping over underbrush, scratching her legs, and tearing her tights. She didn't know where she was going, but she knew no vehicle could follow, and she hoped the guys behind weren't in shape. She heard a gun discharge and a bullet tick through high tree limbs.

This was serious shit.

How long she ran, she could not recall. She finally stopped behind a large ponderosa to listen. The bark smelled like strawberries. Forest sounds—birds and squirrels and wind, but no crunching of footfalls, no ragged breath, save her own.

Now what do I do?

She had no idea how far she had come, which direction was safe, or how she could get back to town without encountering whoever. Then she began to second-guess herself: Were those guys really after me? What did they want? Why me? Who are they? She couldn't describe either one. The guy on the four-wheeler was just a shadow, and the guy by the pickup had on a ball cap and logger clothes, like a hundred other guys around here. He had dark hair. She remembered that.

Some description. Police will have him in no time.

Then she heard a loud CRACK above her, turned, and saw a black shape low to the ground. It rose up, claws embracing a pine. A bear. Oh Jesus. She took off downhill, hair standing up on the back of her neck, zigzagging through the trees. She had read somewhere that you can't outrun a bear, but they have more difficulty running downhill than up. Claws or something. She ran until she came to a clearing, stopped, and listened, too afraid to turn around lest the bear be there, jaws agape.

No bear. More forest sounds.

Where she had stopped was not a meadow. It was a mess. Trees had been cut and dragged recently, but limbs and slash and forest stuff were all over the place, and no attempt at cleanup or forest preservation had been made. Really shoddy work, she thought. Bear or no bear, she was pooped and sat on a stump to recover. "Now all I need is for Bigfoot to drop by." She heard herself say it out loud. The rush of adrenaline and cortisol, or whatever it was, was thumping through her head to the extent that she was vibrating and shaking, so she got off the stump and started looking around. And she thought if they cut trees here they had to drag them somewhere to a road, and a road will get me back to civilization. And then she thought, if this is civilization, I am really in trouble. She walked, not ran.

She did find a road. She looked for the sun. That's east. She crept along, knees slightly bent, ready to dive off into the forest if one of the bad guys, or Bigfoot, or a bear should appear. Give me big city muggers any day of the week. This sucks. The road she was on was small and temporary. It teed into another bigger dirt road. All the roads in the forest looked pretty much the same to her, and there weren't any signs. She turned left because it seemed the more downhill direction. And walked. And came to a paved road. She turned left—it had worked so far. And came to Salish.

Josh Bendix was standing on the porch of the suites when Lara jogged up. "You look like hell, Lara. What happened to you?" Her tights were torn, her face scratched, bits of forest were in her hair like a salad, and her face was flushed bright red.

"I went for a peaceful morning run, was chased by a four-wheeler, jumped over a pickup, was shot at, chased by a bear, and wandered around the forest for god knows how long. Sit tight for a few minutes while I clean up, and I will give you the full story. Better go to your room. It is best not to be hanging around in the open."

"Damnit, Lara," he sputtered, but did what he was told.

CHAPTER 9

Butterflies can taste through their feet.

Sergei (Sam) Ashkenazy had gotten a message to contact Piper Williams. He was solicitous of his clients, but wary. He called, land line to land line. Perhaps it was safer than the new radio phones, he didn't really know, but he would, as always, talk with indirection.

"This is your person for art."

"Yes, Sam, thank you for calling, I have…."

"Wait, please, Missus. You are on land line, yes?"

"Yes, that is right,

"No names, please, although late it is for that. Okay, what I can do?"

"I need you to scout out some more art for my museum. I would prefer some Russian modernists—avant-garde. I like the ones we have purchased before."

"How soon?"

"As soon as possible, but the paint should be dry."

"You are joking me. Please no joke. How many you need?"

"At least three. Same price, okay?"

"I do job. Call you," and he hung up. The call was less than forty seconds.

69

---◆--◆-

SERGEI WAS AN ART CONSULTANT AND ADVISOR. HE HAD contacts throughout the former Soviet Union, and business was good these days for a couple of reasons. Reason number one was that when Russians revolted against the Tzars and then the Bolsheviks took over after World War I, Lenin promoted modern art and a wealth of artists including Kandinsky, Jawlensky, Malevich, Rodchenko and dozens of others, unknown in the West, were cranking out two-dimensional sketches, watercolors, and oil or acrylic paintings. About the time the West took notice, so did Stalin. Stalin was a ruthless son of a bitch with definite ideas and a murderous hand, and he declared Soviet socialist realism the only true and worthwhile art. This drove the modernists underground and much of their work disappeared, stashed in attics, or church basements, or in private collections. Some of these works were reappearing, but they had a big gap in their provenance since they essentially vanished for fifty or sixty years.

The second reason was that when the Soviet Union collapsed just a few years ago, in the early 1990s, so did the funding for some 4,500 art schools throughout the country. Spilling out from this abrupt aesthetic bankruptcy were hundreds—no, thousands—of well-trained and unemployed artists. They were good. You want a Kandinsky? They will make you one and cheap, too. Lissitzky? No problem. Popova? A favorite of mine. I have a whole series of his that the world is soon to discover. They were even good enough that if you wanted a work that was already, inconveniently, owned by a museum, they could make you a really nice copy. No sweat.

Some artworks came out of Russia in diplomatic pouches. Some originals were overpainted, and then the fresh paint removed with solvent when they reached their market. Sergei's job (never Sam when he was doing this) was to authenticate each piece with a believable but totally bogus set of credentials, badges of authority, and phony stories about the miraculous rescue of this priceless work from its obscurity into the wonderful sunlight of the capitalist market. Sergei didn't really care whether a piece was a real Kandinsky or a fake. It was all the same to him.

He knew that Piper Williams didn't care either.

LARA EMERGED FROM THE SHOWER, SCRUBBED BUT scratched. She didn't have any triple antibiotic ointment or bandages, but felt as if she had removed most of the forest. Dark, short hair, wet and cupped around her head, she pounded on Josh's door. He peeked out, let her in, slammed the door.

"Jesus Christ, Lara, you said this wouldn't be dangerous. As you can see my bag is packed, and I would already be in my car miles down the road if I didn't owe you the courtesy of saying I am getting the hell out of here."

"Josh, I need you, but only for today. Hear me out, and then decide if you will help. Will you do that?"

He didn't speak but sat down on the bed looking at the floor between his shoes.

"Josh, you are the only one who knows the Cultural Center's collection. We need to go through it to see what is there and what is missing. Next, we need some more guidance on the financials, mainly where the excess money is coming from and how the federal money has been spent. If you will do those two things for us, then you can beat feet out of here and just wait for a fat check from the NEA. Will you do that?" She grabbed him under the chin and lifted up his face to look him straight in the eyes.

He squirmed. He avoided her eyes, he shook his head sideways, but then nodded twice. She kissed him on the forehead. "You will need to get your slacks and blazer on again, and then the sooner we get to the center, the sooner you will be gone."

<hr />

AT THE CENTER, LARA, JOSH, JUAN OROPALLO, AND THE two US marshals, Lester and Bradley, gathered in the office conference room, and Lara described the excitement of the morning run, gunfire and all. Josh, hearing this for the first time, turned "a whiter shade of pale." The marshals got on the radio and reported the gunshot to the local authorities, describing, as best they could from Lara's vague geography, where it had happened. Searching authorities were unlikely to find more than twenty guys in a ball cap and logger gear.

The marshals said they would keep the logger-guards out of the building, and Lara, Juan, and Josh did an inventory of all the artwork, noting the missing pieces, as before, and listing all those on the walls.

"We don't have an extensive collection, so most of what we have is on display," Josh told them. "But we do have some pieces in storage," and he led them to a room under the massive overhang of the second floor. The office key opened the storage room, and Josh began pawing through the art pieces in the slots against the wall, pulling them out one by one and describing them.

He pulled one out and exclaimed, "Where the hell did this come from?" He pulled out another and another with a stream of expletives that eloquently emphasized his surprise and confusion at the extent of the collection that up to a month before, he had presided over.

"I don't recognize any of these; the style, yes, but they weren't here when I left. Linda McKenzie didn't have the expertise to buy these, or the money either. This is weird."

Lara wrote down the names of the artists. One said W. Kandinsky. Wassily Kandinsky, but wouldn't he have signed his name in Cyrillic? It looked like a Kandinsky. Weird indeed.

———————

Next they went over the books, not just the financials, but the record of contributions, both of money and art, and the logs of purchases. Nothing in the printed documents explained why the center had so much money or where it came from. They were, of course, missing the most recent month's information that would have been on the computers that had vanished. Beyond strange, bordering on what in the military would be a FUBAR.

———————

Josh was anxious to be gone. Lara asked Lester if he could take Josh back to get his car, and then maybe escort him out of town and a few miles down I-5 and alert the state police to watch over him until he reached the California border? That done, Lara called Randall at the NEA to report the excitements of the day and the general state of disarray at the center.

—————•——•——

DID I REALLY SEE A BEAR? LARA'S MIND HAD ITS OWN mind, and sometimes she was not entirely sure who was in control up there in her head-bone. She had grown up in the embrace of the Catholic Church, gone to parochial schools, and been groomed for a life of religious service until she rebelled and thought she had grabbed her life by the scruff of its neck and taken charge. But the religious lessons and discussions and parables and prohibitions kept popping up, unbidden and unwanted, as her mind's mind took charge. She wondered if the bear she had seen was a figment of her imagination. Was there a bear in the woods? (Is the pope Catholic? Does the bear shit in the woods?) She had to find out.

As Lara came through the door of the Forest Service office in Salish, she said: "Mr. Rawlings, you are the first person I met in Salish, and I have a question…is it Mr. Rawlings or Ranger Rawlings?"

"That's your question: am I called Mr. or Ranger?"

"Not really, my mind seems a bit flighty today, but okay, let's start there."

"We're the Forest Service, not Ranger Rick of the comics or some Cub Scout den. Why don't you call me John. And I remember you, pretty lady."

"Are there bears around here?"

"Of course there are bears. That's why all the garbage cans have those funny tops on them. Bears are smart and can figure all sorts of ways of getting at food. They can smell—better than dogs, maybe."

"I got chased by a bear."

"Did you poke him with a stick?"

"No, I was running, you know, out for a morning run, and I got chased by a guy on a four-wheeler, and another guy had a pickup across the road, and I ran through the woods, and then a bear chased…."

"Whoa, whoa, pretty lady. I can see why you came to your favorite body-beautiful, Ranger John, but you need to sit down and have a cup of coffee and talk some sense. Come back here," he said, lifting a portion of the counter and escorting her to a coffee room down the hall.

The coffee was burned and old, but hot. It did some good.

"Now, you say you got chased by a bear?"

"I was running from these two guys."

"What guys?"

"The one on the four-wheeler, and the one with the pickup across the road."

"How do you know they were chasing you?"

"Well shit, John, if you are a female running in the early morning on a deserted road and there are two guys, one coming up from behind and one blocking the road, do you stop and chat them up?"

"I see what you mean. Where was this?"

"It was one of your roads—a Forest Service road, I think, but it didn't have a number on it. Go out of town to the east, and it is about the second one to the right."

"So the bear came up while you were running from these guys?"

This was starting to sound stupid, even to Lara's ears: "No, I bolted off into the forest so the four-wheeler couldn't follow me, and I ran for…I don't know how long…and then I stopped to rest and that is when I saw the bear."

"What color?"

"What color what?

"What color was the bear?"

"Oh, black."

"What was it doing?"

"It was on the ground, and then it stood up and was scratching a tree and at that point I took off and didn't look back."

"Ants. The bear was scratching for ants. They are much tastier than you would have been."

"Bears are dangerous, aren't they?"

"Grizzlies are. They have claws that are five inches long and turn over two-hundred-pound rocks with a single swipe, and they are vicious, but there aren't any grizzlies around here. You have to go to Montana for that."

"No, thank you."

"A momma black bear will give you trouble if you get between her and her cubs, and you want to give them some space, but I seriously doubt that that bear chased you. First, if it had, it would have caught you, and second, it was much more interested in the ants than in you. You aren't supposed to run when you see them, by the way. Stand still and back away slowly."

"Don't worry," said Lara, "I am not going back into the woods. Too dangerous."

"You report those guys that chased you?"

"I did. Do you have any idea who they might have been?"

He didn't.

"Okay, so after I had rested for a while, I was looking around at the clearing where I stopped, and you guys sure made a mess of it when you logged it."

"Here I give you coffee, let you ogle my svelte body while you are spinning your yarn, and now you insult me and my outfit?"

"Well, it was a mess. There were limbs all over the place and scars in the earth, and it looked like somebody just went in there for the big trees and didn't care what happened to the rest."

"Where was this?"

She described it as best she could.

"I bet we have been burgled. We haven't had any sales in that area for years. Timber rustlers. They come in at night, grab the best trees and take off. I had better go take a look."

"Do you know who they were?"

"We have a pretty good idea who it is, but we can never catch them, and whatever timber they steal just disappears. Say, what kind of pickup was it that was across the road?"

Lara didn't know. It was grey, maybe.

Lara thanked him for the coffee. As she was going out the door, he said: "The wife says you ought to talk to this crazy lady that lives around here."

CHAPTER 10

Art is a discipline.
Discipline requires discipline.

———◆———

Lara was back at the Cultural Center. She and Juan had been going through files in the office looking for anything that might be significant. The money that came from the NEA had apparently gone into the center's general account, so it was impossible to tell how or how much of it had been spent without the help of a forensic accountant. For Juan, it was clear that some of the money that came and went was either from or to Williams Lumber, but again, he was not skilled enough to establish a definitive trail, let alone one that would be actionable. What Juan was doing, in a semi-annoying way, was constructing limericks. His latest was about the logger-guards:

> They've got the boots and the suspenders,
> And the trucks with rusted fenders.
> But when it comes to art,
> They just ain't that smart,
> Cause God put their brains in a blender.

Lara tried to ignore him. Then she sighed and said, "Open up your wallet and hand over your poetic license. I am revoking it."

Lester wandered in to check on how they were doing. He said Bradley was keeping an eye on the loggers, and he wanted a cup 'o joe. Would they care to join him?

"No, Juan, don't recite your latest limerick for him. Have some self-respect."

This, of course, demanded a recitation, that produced a smile and nod from Lester, who then said to Lara: "Could you give me a guided tour of this place? I don't know anything about art, but I find some of these pieces confusing, and if you have time, you could educate me."

"I bet you know a whole lot more than you think you do," said Lara, "and I would be delighted. Want to do it right now?"

Taking his arm, she led him to the first gallery. "First thing to know is that what is valuable in art doesn't always translate into words. Art is personal and at the same time universal, at least good art is. Just because you don't relate to a piece the first time you see it doesn't mean it is bad art or that you are a Philistine. It is sort of like a courtship—it takes time, and you may never fall in love, but when you do, your beloved will shower you with gifts of beauty and insight for a lifetime.

"Here is a work by Childe Hassam painted in the early 20th century. The first thing you ask yourself is, what is the artist's perspective? Is he far or near, a part of what he has selected to show us, or outside of it? What time of day is it; where are the shadows? Is the artist telling us a story, and if so, are we meant to be a part of it? Does the painting have internal consistency, that is, if it is meant to be realistic, is it? Are the hands out of proportion; is the perspective unpersuasive? Then notice how the artist uses the materials with which the work is made: Is the surface smooth or bumpy; is it shiny or dull? Why did the artist make it that way?

"Hassam was a great fan of nature, and he shows tremendous respect for the mountains of the Pacific Northwest. He is famous enough that I am surprised that this museum could find a piece of his to buy, and afford it if they did."

"So where do paintings like this come from?" asked Lester.

"Auction houses mainly. Christie's and Sotheby's, Bonhams in San Francisco. There are lots, but the really high-end works don't come up very often. The other big source is private collectors who donate to the museum. I would expect that this Cultural Center has some collectors they are courting, but they are into the game late, and their chance of getting an old master like a Rembrandt or a European impressionist like Monet are virtually nil."

"When you say 'impressionist,' what do you mean?"

"It is a dumb thing the art world does. Artists and especially art critics and art scholars are not immune from pretention, and they try to put artists and artworks in boxes. It is a fool's errand because, if it is any good, every artwork is unique. It is its own definition.

"But over the years there have been eight or so art movements starting with Japanese woodblocks to romanticism, impressionism, and cubism where the works, even rendering of the human figure, are in geometric shapes. Bauhaus, mostly in Germany between the world wars, is another where the figures are disconnected and the colors unexpected. Bauhaus annoyed Hitler and he tried to snuff it, and its proponents out. There are a couple more schools I am forgetting, but the artists who are catalogued that way have certain similarities in style, in artists whom they have studied with or copied, or in the timeframe in which they worked. It is pretty arbitrary, but it is a useful shorthand."

"But you didn't answer my question," Lester said. "What does impressionist mean?"

"I'll answer a question with a question: When you get an impression of something, what do you mean?"

"I get a sense of something, but it is imprecise?"

"Exactly. The subjects of the work are obscure; the edges fuzzy; the perspectives out of kilter. Many of the impressionists were influenced by Asian art, particularly Japanese woodblock prints. It is a fusion of artistic styles in a way similar to what jazz has done with music from all over the globe."

They moved on to another gallery, and Lara stopped near the door. "Okay, Lester, just take a 360-degree look around this gallery and pick out two works you want to talk about. If you try to absorb everything in a museum, you will go into artistic overload, and your eyeballs will start spinning and your head will pop.

"Good choice. This is C.S. Price. He and a lot that followed him were beholden to the Federal Art Project during the Depression. The government paid artists a living wage, and they produced some marvelous work, and as far as I understand the art scene in the Northwest, generations of artists have learned from and emulated those easel painters of the 1930s. C.S. Price is the big daddy of that group, and I am really surprised they could find and acquire one. What do you think of it?"

"Why is everything in the picture gold?"

"Partly style, partly trying to create a mood, or trick the eye, but remember, the artist doesn't own the painting after it goes into the public domain, and often the artist is the last person to be able to explain what it is or what it means. And since you as the viewer—the consumer—bring your own perspective, your own life—to the viewing, what it says to you is what it means. If you come back tomorrow, or next week or ten years from now it might mean something different. I would hope so."

They came to a color field of vertical stripes by Gene Davis. "This looks like one of those black and white blocks of stripes, I think they call them bar codes, that they scan to tell how much something costs, except it is in color," Lester said. "Why is this good?"

"This is going to sound like a cop-out, but one answer is, it is good because it is in a museum. It is like saying, I am famous for being famous. But there is some truth to the answer, namely, that some people on a collection committee, professionals who have spent their lives studying art, think it is good. Art should make us stretch; it should challenge us. If an artwork gives up all of its mysteries the first time you see it, it probably is schlock, and if you bought it and took it home you would hate it tomorrow, and it would be in the trash next Wednesday. With color fields and geometrics, they are challenging your eyes, so you have to look at them for a long time and let them absorb you. Come back, when you have time, and just look at this one and let it eat you up."

They traversed several more galleries and from the comments Lester made, it was clear to Lara that his powers of observation were keen and his eye sophisticated. Then she thought that he was, after all, a law enforcement officer and they were, as a profession, professional information gatherers. They were taught to be keen observers. Cool.

In one of the bigger galleries, Lester stopped before a painting of figures done by Russian artist Natalia Goncharova. "I like this one because it is done by a woman."

"Well, gender alone wouldn't get a woman into a museum, but for centuries, it kept them out. Women couldn't act in plays, for a long time, they couldn't even sing the high parts—boys did that—it has been a stinky world for women to create in."

"Look at the faces," Lester said. "They all kind of look the same, and the figures are fuzzy and the tree doesn't look much like a tree, but I like it and it has a lot of truth in it. How did she do that?"

"Ah, the mystery. If I could tell you that, Lester, well, I wouldn't want to be able to tell you, because the mystery is the punch behind the paint. This is a woman who died at age 35, but she not only broke the gender barrier, she was a genius. Died of scarlet fever, I think." Lara looked at the small plaque by the painting. It said she died in 1962. "No, I am gassing you and am caught in my own pretension. That was another Russian woman of the avant-garde school, named Lyubov Popova.

"You can see that I am an unreliable guide, but look, Lester, at the one next to it. Same artist, Goncharova, but what she has done with the guy on the bicycle is to stack images on each other like frames in a motion picture."

"I've seen one like this before," said Lester. "It was hanging in that big mansion. I saw it while we were waiting for the reluctant but haughty lady to get us a key for this place."

LARA WAS SITTING IN THE SINGLE CHAIR IN HER "SUITE" of a single room; well, it had a bathroom, maybe that made it a suite. Anyway, she was reflecting on the art tour she had given Lester and trying to sort things out when her mind's mind trotted out some more intellectual thuggery. It was part of her "interiority complex": a mind that kept asking questions her brain could not answer.

What would happen if we were governed by the power of art rather than the power of weapons and physical intimidation? It would be the power to create rather than the power to destroy. Power, in an aesthetic sense isn't about one individual imposing his will on another, but about each individual seeking, and hopefully finding, a muse—a spiritual guide to the realm of beauty and human fulfillment. That could be the definition of true freedom.

Yeah, but (her mind's mind had a grand inquisitor) deception is the stock and trade of the artist, not just the fiction writer, but the composer who seeks mystery, the painter who tricks our vision, the poet whose meaning (or the lack thereof) creates a metaphor—a lie that is a lie, rather than a lie that is true.

Art (said the rejoinder of her hopeful mind) has the ability to create a dynamic relationship with the viewer. It is a dialogue between the past and present, and it can affect the future. What that means is that art can be the intermediary that shows us who and where we are and helps us discover what we should and can be, both individually and as a society.

What a bunch of unadulterated crap (this is the grand inquisitor). Art is not going to change human nature and humans are a flawed species. The only power they know is physical power and that is why they have been killing each other since the beginning of time. Art isn't going to change that.

Art exemplifies the aesthetic of care (her positive mind was still trying). It uses vulnerability as a weapon, if you will. So if art, say a poem or a play, shows how one person can care for, help, empathize with, and support another, isn't that a recipe for community?

Not in a world full of guns and angry people.

But that is exactly the point. One person with a gun will eventually run out of bullets, but one person with a song….

Lara shook her head. Kumbaya is not the answer. I have got to do something; that or go home.

Like what?

Her mind's mind wasn't done.

Perhaps the value of art is that it disperses power; its meaning is owned by no one. Uncertainty of meaning gives art its power, and art doesn't need an organizing principle because it belongs to everybody. Art rather than war can be the hygiene of the world. Art as service; art as gift; art as community.

Gotta go, gotta go. She got up and went out, car keys in hand, with no destination in mind.

———◆———

She started up the grade, past the Forest Service office, without a clear idea of where the road went. She tooled along, mind in neutral, replaying the discussion her mind had just had. It was pleasant. She had had this discussion with herself before and knew it wouldn't be resolved, but it was useful just to think. Thinking as a hobby.

What about a pipe organ or a guitar? Do fine instruments have all manner of tunes and harmonies locked in them just waiting for a human to come along and caress them; coax them out? Wonderful notes and sonorities and passions? Then she fantasized about the singer, tidy-tushed guy at the presentable dive. What would happen if they…?

It wasn't a sound she could remember that jolted her out of her reverie; it was a sixth sense that something had intruded, and that intrusion was in the form of a grey pickup that was a few feet from her back bumper.

She floored it.

It, the car, reluctantly sped up drawing a few feet away from the pickup, but not shooting out like a gazelle.

Oh help.

She didn't know where she was going, what kind of road it was, or if there were any towns. She looked in her mirror. Two shapes in the front seat of the truck.

These had to be the same guys, and they had a gun then. Now, they probably have ten guns.

She flashed her lights wildly at an oncoming car. It flashed back. Communication without content.

Think. I have a little more than half a tank of gas. If I just keep driving, keep ahead of them, what? What if this road just ends? What if I get myself so far into the mountains that nobody ever finds me? Where can I find help?

CHAPTER 11

Towers are for men; spires are for God.

A board foot is the equivalent of a slab of wood one inch thick, twelve inches long, and twelve inches wide, or 144 cubic inches of product. It is the measure, usually in millions of board feet, of output from a mill. The profitability of a mill depends on the market price of the finished lumber less the cost of the raw material (the logs), the cost of the labor (the loggers, trucks, machinery, mill workers, and maintenance), and administrative and fixed costs (buildings, land, taxes, etc.).

When logs arrive at a mill, they have to be scaled to estimate their value. The easiest, and least exact way, to do this is to weigh the loaded log truck, remove the logs, and weigh the truck again. You then have the weight of the logs, but not all logs are created equal. Not all logs are straight, not all logs are rot free, not all logs have the same taper…you get the idea.

A return to log calculation tells the mill owner whether he (always he) will make money on a given log or group of logs, or all the logs in a given month or year. All this is inexact for the already stated reasons, namely that log shape, sweep and crook, density, moisture content, checks, taper, and the eyeball of the scaler person vary.

The taper end of the log is measured inside the bark. The bark doesn't produce any board feet, and there is additional loss to kerf (from the blade of the saw that results in sawdust), the slabbing of the bark to get the log square, the edging, the shrinkage, and all of that stuff that used to get burned up in wigwam burners—those things that looked like a giant thimble on its base with a screen across the top and all manner of smoke and pollutants streaming out the top twenty-four hours a day. Those things used to be the hallmark of loggerdom. Any forest guy worth his salt loved to see the flames coming out the top against the night sky.

Edward Doyle created a formula for calculating the board foot return from a log sometime before the Civil War. The equation had the diameter and length, with some factors divided by sixteen. It was a measure, but an imprecise one. A guy named Scribner (good name for a lad who wrote things down) had a more complicated scale in which he took a fraction of the diameter and length to account for waste, and this formula was further modified to the Scribner Decimal C Rule. All of this makes one's head hurt, and it didn't matter anyway for one simple reason: the folks at Williams Lumber, well, one of them at least, didn't give a shit about the quality of these logs because they were free.

Piper Williams didn't, on the other hand, give a rat's ass about what went on at Williams Lumber as long as the money kept pouring in. And it arrived by the bucket full.

So what did she do all day in that Victorian mansion? She started with a workout in the fully equipped gym in the basement. She did free weights, lying on a bench on her stomach and lifting with her arms to tone the shoulders; on her back to tone the arms. She did power lifts for leg strength with the butler spotting for her. She ran on the treadmill; did the stair machine. She even rowed the Concept II ergometer—a rowing machine designed by a diabolical torturer. She dripped sweat in a most unladylike fashion, using towel after towel handed by the butler, and dropped after each wipe. When she had finished her routine, she stepped into the open shower, shed her workout clothes, and let the water carry away the heat of her body. The butler stayed around should he be needed.

After the workout came her minimal breakfast. Eating was a bother. She didn't enjoy it and only did so because she had to. Then came her "toilet" where she stood in front of a mirror and took stock of her equipment. Her chin was strong, but not a Hapsburg ship's brow. It was an "I will not be denied" chin.

The line of her face was straight, not curved. Curves can be beautiful and soft. Straight was imperial and demanding. Her hair was black—not brown black or red black or grey black but black like "black is the color of my true love's hair"—and her eyes were, too. Black as Erebus. Her skin was uncommonly white, and she searched it for bumps or god forbid, a mole or blemish or fugitive hair.

At five foot nine inches tall, she was strong; handsome strong. All of her pieces fit together, and she kept them well pampered. She flew to San Francisco monthly for her haircut. She had all the lotions and oils and powders that could have been brought from exotic and ancient places by camel caravan. When she walked into a room, folks noticed, except she never walked, she processed as a royal among her subjects.

The daily toilet completed; she sat down to take stock of things. Things took the form of objects. Things took the form of people who could do things for her. And things took the form of money, of which a lot was never enough.

She was an arithmomaniac—one with an uncontrollable urge to calculate numbers. She knew how much money she had to the nearest nickel, and her greatest daily pleasure was to do the math that told her how much more she had today than yesterday.

Legend has it that vampires, like Dracula, are arithmomaniacs.

As Lara drove, gas pedal flattened against the firewall, she tried to read the license plate on the truck. It was backwards in the mirror and too bouncy, and if she didn't figure out some way to get these assholes off her tail, she was toast anyway. What to do? She rounded another curve on the two lane, increasingly steep asphalt road. The shoulders were a narrow ditch and beyond that, the pines were consistently dense and lethal. If she went off the road she would hit a tree and that would be the last of her. The truck had more power than her rental and on the increasing grade was closing fast.

In the distance, maybe a quarter mile, an oncoming car rounded a corner, and she thought she saw the gumball antlers that might be a bar of emergency lights. Time for some decisive action. She swerved into the oncoming lane, blinking her lights furiously. The truck had come abreast of her, and she saw the dark-haired driver grinning out his side window.

She was now boxed in. She slammed on the brakes as the oncoming car activated its emergency lights with the nose of the car diving as it braked violently. Time slowed down as Lara's car skidded straight, the oncoming car slewed to the left almost sideways, regained control and slewed to the right blocking both lanes and sending up a cloud of blue smoke as the pavement abraded the tires. It stopped five feet in front of her. The side of the car, still rocking from the inertia, had a big star that said Douglas County Sheriff.

The truck slammed on its brakes, lost the rear end, and slewed sideways, half on and half off the pavement. And there they were, just a few feet apart, all stopped.

The two guys were first out of their vehicle. Lara made sure her doors were locked, put the car in reverse just in case, and waited for the deputy sheriff to get out. He just sat there, apparently calling on his radio, while the two logger guys in ball caps, hands in pockets, loitered around the deputy's door. Then the deputy got out, and they shook hands! Oh, mother of god; they know each other. Should she flee? The logger guys were talking and gesturing and pointing at Lara and obviously spinning some tale in which she was the bad actor and they were the upstanding, hardworking, salt of the earth locals who just happened to witness whatever vile deed she had supposedly perpetrated.

She sat. She watched. She waited.

Eventually, the deputy nodded, the logger guys got back in their truck, backed farther into the ditch, spun their back tires churning up a cloud of dust, shifted into four-wheel drive, and peeled out back toward town.

The deputy walked slowly toward her car, hand resting lightly on the butt of his weapon. He had reddish hair, cut

high and tight Marine style, military pressed shirt, obligatory aviator shades although it was almost dark.

She made herself small in the seat.

He tapped on her window. She rolled it down a couple
of inches. His name tag said Plug. Her mind's mind kicked
in: what kind of a name is Plug? She looked again. It was
Pflug. She willed her mind to knock it off.

"Step out of your car, please Ma'am."

"Those guys were chasing me, officer."

"I said, step out of your car. Do it now."

"What did they tell you? They were chasing me, and a
couple of days ago they chased me in the woods and shot
at me. Why did you let them go?"

"This is your last warning. Out of the car, now."

She got out. She was trembling, fear and her exploding
anger pulsing through her brain, her muscles, her bones.

"Keep your hands where I can see them, turn around,
spread your feet, and place both hands on the car."

Her mind's mind suggested she ask him how she could
both keep her hands in sight and turn around, but being a
smart ass was a really bad idea in these circumstances, so
she did as told, just like she had seen in one hundred cop
shows on TV.

He gave her the pat-down, and to her surprise, did not
add an unscheduled bit of molestation or an extra errant
squeeze in her strategic parts. He then ordered her to turn
around, spread her arms wide, close her eyes, and slowly
bring her hand in and touch her nose. She tried, but her
hand was shaking and she missed her nose and poked her
cheek. He then told her to walk a straight line on the pavement putting one foot, heel to toe in front of the other. She
wobbled. She swayed.

"Turn around, Ma'am, and put your hands behind your back." He cuffed her. "I am taking you in for driving under the influence and reckless driving." Then he took out a card and read her her rights.

She would remain silent now, but she would scream bloody murder later.

SHE WAS BOOKED INTO THE JAIL IN ROSEBURG, FINGER-printed, her shoes, belt, and personal items removed and catalogued, given some creepy jail slippers, and locked up.

No phone call until tomorrow, she was told.

No reason was given.

CHAPTER 12

A well-ordered life might be just plain dull.

"I'm in jail. Can you come and get me?"

"Lara, Lara, what have you gotten yourself into this time?" George Graham, her FBI surrogate dad, was on the other end of the line.

"I am totally innocent. Yah, yah, I know everyone tells you that, but it happens to be true. I was chased when I was running in the woods, and today, I was in my car and the same guys were chasing me in a pickup. I stopped a sheriff's deputy by swerving into his lane. He knew the guys in the pickup. He let them go and arrested me. This is not a friendly place."

"Where are you?"

"Roseburg. It is a town on I-5 about halfway down the state. Do you have any FBI guys here who can get me out?"

"Try to understand, Sweetie, that we are not a bail bond agency. Can't you tell them what happened. Were there witnesses?"

"No witnesses except the guys who were chasing me, and they were smiling when they thought I was going to head-on the deputy. Bad guys."

"What about the local district attorney?"

"Well, whoever that is hasn't dropped by to see me in my jail cell. In fact, I have been in here over twelve hours, and no one has talked to me except to bring some food-like stuff."

"What do you want me to do about it, Lara?"

"Jesus, I don't know. I have never been in jail before. I don't know anybody out here. My NEA contacts are arts administrators, not jailhouse lawyers."

"I will see what I can do. Don't talk to anybody—I mean don't give any statement or interview to any law enforcement type—I can't believe I am saying this. Just sit tight. Is there a way I can call you?"

"They took all my personal stuff. My big brick of a mobile phone is in my motel room. Call the Roseburg jail, I guess. And thank you, George. I am sorry to be trouble."

"You are nothin' but trouble, Sweat Pea."

———◆———

Juan Oropallo wondered what the hell had happened to Lara. His "suite" was right next to hers, but she wasn't there and neither was her car. He hung around until about midmorning and then went to the Cultural Center. Bradley and Lester were there, but strangely enough, the logger-guards were not.

Bradley and Lester didn't know where Lara was either.

Juan spent a few unproductive hours looking at financial documents, got hungry, and decided he would schlep down to the tavern for a burger. There was an old guy hunched over the bar staring at his beer. Juan slid onto the stool next to him, ordered a coke, got a Pepsi, and waited to see if the guy could talk.

No talk.

Bartender came back and Juan ordered, upon recommendation, a smash burger.

Extended silence.

The beer on the bar was three quarters full; its drinker, catatonic. Maybe he was dead and stuffed just so it would look like the bar had some patrons. Juan remembered a place that advertised snakes that it hoped folks would pay to look at near his childhood home in Southern Oregon. Nobody in his right mind would patronize the place, but the proprietor put an old Cadillac with a flat tire out front to suggest somebody was stupid enough to stop.

"Sheriff arrested somebody."

Juan wasn't sure if the comment was directed at him, or even if it came from the frozen drinker because he didn't see the guy's mouth move. He waited.

"Practically had a head-on, way I heard it."

"Really?" Juan had a way with words.

Silence.

His smash burger arrived.

"Up the road toward Fall Creek Falls."

Is that the best they could do for a name? thought Juan.

More silence. The beer remained at three quarters.

"Lady was drunk."

Juan ventured a question: "How did you find this out?"

No answer.

Smash burger was good. Conversation, if that is what it could be called, flagged. Flagged some more. Was over. Glass still registered three-fourths full. A limerick popped into Juan's head. He couldn't help it:

> I'm sittin' here listenin' to nothin'.
> The guy next to me's filled with stuffin'.

Says a lady was drunk,
Goes back to his funk,
And I'm eating some meat on a muffin.

JUAN, BEING A PROFESSIONAL INVESTIGATOR AND ALL, wondered if the drunk lady his comatose bar friend had mentioned was real or a figment of the guy's addled mind. Since he didn't have much else to do at the Cultural Center, he thought he would spool on down to Roseburg and check things out. He called the attorney general's office to report what he had found so far (not much) and told them where he was going. His supervisor said that the DA in Douglas County was a friend of hers and to drop in and see him. His name was Jim Stetson, you know, like the hat.

Downtown Roseburg was semi-depressing to Juan. Every other storefront seemed to be empty or selling used stuff. There were some massive chainsaw benches with Ronald Reagan's face carved on them—a chance to sit with Ronnie—used golf clubs, lamps without shades, bowling balls, old suitcases. Stuff upon stuff. Juan knew of the explosion fifty years ago. It looked as if they never rebuilt. They should have taken that urban architect up on his offer to make it a showplace. He couldn't even find a plaque commemorating the big KA-BOOM.

The courthouse was nice, a kind of low-slung Greco-Roman number with six columns, double rows of windows, and a top balustrade reminiscent of the White House. He went in, was directed to the district attorney's office, and had a nice chat with Jim Stetson. Stetson was in his third term as DA, and probably could stay forever if he wanted. There wasn't much crime around. Well, there was lots of rural thievery and marijuana growing and poverty-driven desperation, but apprehensions were few, and frankly, Jim was a little bored.

Juan told Stetson what he was doing in Salish. Stetson listened intently, seemed as if he was about to comment, and then just shook his head. They shook hands and parted. Juan drove around Roseburg for a while and then back to Salish. Stetson hadn't known anything about a specific drunk lady. There were quite a few of them around.

LARA LEARNED, BY READING A SIGN IN THE JAIL, THAT she could receive three pairs of socks and three bras (no underwires) every ninety days. Also permitted were prescription glasses and medical necessities. Clergy could bring "religious books of authority." She had had just about enough of authority in any guise— any manifestation. She had dumped her religion a long time ago, although like a malignant wart, it kept reappearing through her mind's mind and tweaking her on the conscience about jettisoning the "one true faith." In jail with nothing to do, she still was too busy to revisit those struggles of doubt and faith, and as far as she was concerned, there was no "religious book of authority" that could impose its will over her.

The jail signs also told her, authoritatively, that inmates could work—in the kitchen, cleaning the facility, doing clerical tasks. No violent crimes inmates would qualify; drug tests would be administered. No persons with TB. Work cleaning the highways (the chain gang?) was only for those already sentenced. Presumably brownie points would be awarded, but the sign did not explain.

She thought, if I am in here long enough to find out, I won't have a mind to worry about.

———◆——

"I'm your lawyer," the lady said looking through the bars.

She had a pretty face atop a very tall body. Dressed in blue jeans, boots, a man's work shirt, long brown hair pulled back in a ponytail, she cleared six feet, was fully filled out in proportion to her size, and stood, one hip cocked to the side, as if she were about to swing a lariat. The ponytail shot straight out backwards, like the flames from an afterburner. Let loose, her hair had its own zip code.

Lara was drowsy—disoriented from her mostly sleepless night on the thing with mattress ticking cloth but no padding that flopped on the shelf that served as a bed, and her mind's mind was still pondering "books of authority."

"I'm Marcia Stone. Call me Stoney. Some guy named Graham called me from back east and said you were in trouble. He your dad?" Stoney had been everything from a belly dancer to a rescue ranger in the Jefferson wilderness. Once she even rescued a boy who had fallen in a slippery waterfall. There was snow and she was wearing flip-flops, no less. Well, her boots hurt, and she didn't feel like putting them back on.

"No, he is a special agent for the FBI. He and I are friends," said Lara as she got up off the cot and moved toward the bars.

"Not a bad friend to have. He wants me to get you out of here. Said he would pay my fee. I charge the rock bottom rate of $110 per hour, and you get your money's worth because in this backwater of male chauvinism, a girl has to kick some serious butt to get noticed, and I have my boots on."

"Do we have to talk through the bars? Isn't there some place more private, more comfortable?"

Stoney put a finger to either side of her mouth and emitted a shrill whistle, followed by: "Dudley, you worthless piece of shit, get down here and unlock this cell."

He did, and they sat side by side on the bench/bed as Lara explained what had happened.

Stoney asked questions but took no notes. When Lara was done, Stoney said, "Okay."

"Okay, what?"

"Okay, I am on it." And she whistled again for the piece of shit to let her out.

CHAPTER 13

It is not a problem
if I solve it.

Douglas County DA Jim Stetson, while bored with his day-to-day administrative tasks and lack of arrests for the petty crimes that rural areas seemed to foment, did get his juices flowing when a murder came his way. Now that the victim had been identified as Linda McKenzie, all he needed was for a killer to show up. Then he could have a whiz-bang trial and get lots of good publicity. What fun. He loved performing in the courtroom; trial preparation, on the other hand, was a bitch. His favorite case, five, no, seven years ago, was the murder of a guy who was driving a road grader with his girlfriend sitting on his lap. His wife shot him dead and was proud to say so.

He went down to talk to the sheriff to see if there were any new leads. There weren't. What was most frustrating was that the perpetrator(s)—perps—were rubbing it in their faces by dumping the casket with Linda's body in the cemetery. Beyond rude. That had to be some kind of message, but the intended recipient of that message and its intended content were both a mystery.

He didn't have anything else to do so he put on his suit coat, went to his car, and drove out to The Left Coast Cultural Center to see if anybody there had some clues about dead Linda. High goats—the weather would be fine.

What a surprise. The place was guarded by two US marshals looking as if they, too, didn't have enough to do. Why wasn't I told about this? He was standing there being educated on the travails of the Cultural Center when his new friend from the attorney general's office, Juan Oropallo, joined the party and offered to show him around. Juan had mentioned earlier that he was looking for his "colleague" who was out here from the National Endowment. Stetson may not have been the brightest crayon in the box, but Linda McKenzie being killed and this NEA lady missing— was that a clue?

Oropallo explained to Stetson that the computers were all gone, that there was more money in the center's accounts than there should be, and that Piper Williams, who was the only functioning trustee, was exquisitely unhelpful.

At the mention of Piper Williams, Stetson visibly winced.

"What?" asked Juan.

"Everywhere, everything, all the time, that's what," Stetson said. "Everything that happens in the county, good, bad, or indifferent, is twice as hard to deal with because the Williamses—Bill the pope and Piper the pope-ette—have to be consulted, stroked, cajoled, and satisfied before anything can be done. I try to stay as far away from them as I can, but it is a small place, and their tenacles are everywhere."

"Are they corrupt?" asked Juan.

"I don't know if they pay their taxes or if they hire undocumented helpers, but on the surface they are as upstanding and civic-minded as Caesar's wife."

"Would you ask around, please, and see if you can find out where Lara Cole went? She has been missing for a whole day, and given the creepy stuff that is going on around here, I am worried."

"What creepy stuff? Do you mean too much money?"

"That and artwork the former director couldn't identify, pictures that have been taken off the wall and are missing, and Lara being chased and shot at by some guys in the woods."

"WHAT?"

"A couple of days ago, she was running on a Forest Service road and two guys, one on a four-wheeler and one with a pickup across the road, tried to grab her. She is a runner and got away by darting off through the woods, but she heard a shot and the bullet going through the treetops."

"She told you this when?"

"Two days ago."

"Is she believable?"

"Absolutely. I saw her just as she came back. She was scratched and flushed in the face and scared as hell."

"I'll see what I can find out." And he left, no, he ran to his car and peeled out.

THREE SEPARATELY CRATED PARCELS ARRIVED AT THE Victorian mansion that afternoon. The butler hefted them inside. Piper wanted them unpacked so she could inspect the merchandise before she decided what to do with them.

One she liked and thought she had a place where it would go nicely. The other two would serve her purposes, as those before had done. She authorized payment to Sam in the usual fashion.

All in a day's work.

LARA WAS GETTING PRETTY GODDAMNED TIRED OF BEING in jail.

She had tried mind control and failed at that. She had sung some songs to herself, but that didn't help for long. She ran and reran the chase and arrest in her mind, trying to figure out if she could have done anything differently; trying to understand how she became the criminal, and the thugs got a walk. Now she had two felonies charged against her: reckless driving and driving under the influence. That is what the ticket said. Stoney had taken it, telling Lara that the DA would have to indict her.

Was Stoney for real, or just another enigma in an increasingly confusing place?

If she were in here long enough to get three bras (without underwires), she would surely lose her mind. She willed herself to be with Michael. Doing what? Just being grounded and comforted. Being folded into a mystic place. Being filled with a peace that prayer, for her, had never achieved. It was beautiful notwithstanding her venue. Her mind also flicked to the image of the sexy minstrel guy in the clean, presentable dive-tavern. No disrespect to Michael's memory. Life goes on. Whereupon, the residual guilt of her Catholic upbringing raised its finger of shame. She clamped her jaws on it like a rabid dog and shook until it disappeared.

STONEY WAS SITTING IN JIM STETSON'S OFFICE CHAIR, with her boots on the desktop when he returned.

"Your guys fucked up, Stetson, but I am going to give you an opportunity to avoid getting your ass kicked, again."

"Nice to see you too, Stoney. Get out of my chair."

She swung her legs off the desk, rose, and as she passed him coming around the desk observed, out loud, that he was getting a little sparse in the hair department.

She sat down and gave him the stink-eye.

"What?"

She gave more stink-eye. Said nothing.

"OK, I'm intimidated. Tell me why you are here or get the hell out of my office."

"I am here because you have a lady in your jail who was chased by some local thugs, not once but twice, and who are, apparently, intent on killing her. The brain-dead deputy who arrested her let the thugs go—he probably knows them. I want you to go with me right now, down to your jail, and talk to her. Otherwise, my next stop is your favorite reporter at the local fish wrapper."

"Who is this lady?"

"She is a very nice person who was sent out here by the National Endowment for the Arts to check out the doings of the Left Coast Cultural Center, and I am hired, by the way, by none other than Special Agent George Graham of the Federal Bureau of Investigation. You may know them as the FBI."

"Why does this stuff happen to me?"

HAVING TALKED TO LARA IN HER CELL AFTER BEING LET in, and out, by deputy shit-piece, Stoney and DA Stetson were now sitting in the office of the sheriff, an elected official. The sheriff was showing dark sweat stains on the underarms of his khaki military press shirt. A fuckup was at hand. Deputy sheriff Jason Pflug was also there. He still had red hair, now accompanied by a very red face.

Juan Oropallo had been called and joined the festivities. While this was ostensibly about Lara, he couldn't keep his eyes off Stoney. What a specimen of female pulchritude! She made his blood migrate.

Juan confirmed that Lara had been chased in the forest. Stoney cross-examined Pflug about what the two thugs told him, whether he knew them, why he let them go, why he didn't take a statement from Lara, what his notebook said (he had neglected to write up the arrest), why not—wasn't that standard procedure? And so on. He was evasive, then hostile, then contrite. He had screwed up big time.

"But she almost crashed into me," he whined.

Juan looked upon Stoney's performance with mouth agape. This was a wonderful woman.

She had destroyed any case Douglas County had against Lara, and it was now time for damage control since Lara could sue the pants off them for all manner of false imprisonment and collect big bucks.

Stetson made the charges of reckless driving and DUI go away, the sheriff himself with a contrite Deputy Pflug went to Lara's cell, apologized profusely, got her car out of hock, and hoped to hell she was not of the vindictive ilk.

Oropallo asked Stoney if she was free for dinner.

CHAPTER 14

Love affairs, like wars, are easier to start than end.

B ill Williams made it his business to know everything that was going on in his sphere of influence. He had a lot of influence. He was the pope, after all.

He was happy enough to have the woman from DC in jail. He had made it known that delay in processing her was desirable. The pope did not explain; he decreed. Now that she was out and about, however, what he wanted was for the DC lady to go home, the other snoops from the AG's office to bug out, and the Cultural Center to open back up under some kind of new management—management that his wife, Piper, could control. The Cultural Center was, whether others acknowledged it or not, an integral part of his life because, for the most part, it kept his wife occupied.

The NEA grant had been a mistake. He knew that now and kicked himself for not paying more attention. Audits were fine as long as he, the pope, got to choose the auditor. Others poking around in the center's records was not acceptable. The center was Piper's show, and Piper did exactly as she pleased. Generally accepted accounting principles uniformly applied would not have crossed her mind.

He got on the horn and started calling important people: the governor, the state's two US senators, his congressman. The message was the same in each call: Both the state and the feds are poking around in my Cultural Center, rudely and unnecessarily. I support you because you get things done. What needs to be done here is for this crap to stop. Got it? Of course, he was polite and low key. No raised voices, no overt threats, no promises of future contributions and political support, but the message was clear, unmistakable, and curt.

Everyone knew the pope kept score.

RANDALL FROM THE NEA HAD LEFT MULTIPLE MESSAGES on Lara's phone-brick while she was in the slammer. The earliest messages wanted her to report progress. The middle messages wanted to know where she was and why she wasn't calling back, and the last messages told her "things had changed" and she should call him right away. He reminded her that it was not Lara-like to be unresponsive.

She needed a shower first to wash off as much of the jail as she could. Then she needed a drink. She went to the tavern, ordered a bourbon on the rocks in a paper cup, brought it back to her suite, and then called Randall. It being three hours later in DC, he had gone home. She left a message, basically saying: thanks a lot for being so helpful while I was put in jail trying to do your work. She didn't say "up yours," but the message she left was pregnant.

She finished the bourbon and went back to the tavern for dinner. It was packed. She sat at a table by herself, and locals kept stopping by to congratulate her on the butt-kicking she—well actually Stoney—had delivered to "the man." Drinks kept arriving unbidden from unknown admirers, and she kept drinking them. As the night wore on, she moved to a larger table where, with much alcohol fueled hilarity, stories were screamed above the din about loggers stealing trees, accountants cooking books, law enforcement taking bribes, and people getting shot.

Lara benefited from an alcoholic haze or all of the talk would have really freaked her out.

"Mondegreens!" shouts a thoroughly besotted patron.

Cheers go up all around.

"What's that?" asks Lara, ready to play, but clueless of the game.

Misheard song lyrics, they tell her. Start with the easy ones on Christmas songs. But remember, it doesn't count unless you sing it.

"Olive, the other reindeer." Chorus of boos.

"Round John Virgin, motherless child/ Wholly infantile, totally wild." Applause for a patron who can hold it together for two lines.

"Gladly, the cross-eyed bear." Yah, yah. Get some new material.

"Here's the one you have all been waiting for." Then singing badly: "The cattle are lonely, the poor baby waves." More boos.

"Good King Wences's car backed out/ On a piece of Stephen." Lots of heard it befores.

Woman climbs awkwardly onto the table, sways with hand over heart, and recites: "I led the pigeons to the flag/ of the United States of America." Cheers and salutes, particularly as her dress flairs up as she is hauled down from the table. Somebody yells, "America, America, God is Chef Boyardee."

Without gaining the floor, besotted patrons, in what would hardly be called a Greek chorus, chant, "Sweet dreams are made of cheese," and "Feelin' the beat of the tangerine," and "This is the dawning of the age of asparagus." Two guys, shuffling and snapping fingers: "I've got two chickens to paralyze."

Next victim, they shout. Lara, Lara, Lara.

Lara has the hang of it by now, although, sober, she never would have participated. Sober, she was not. Singing, sort of: "Every time you go away/ you take a piece of meat with you." Atta girls all around.

"The ants are my friends." Tunelessly presented. What? they shout. Then someone sings it—just three descending notes—Blowin' in the Wind.

General hilarity and disorder.

Tapping on a glass for attention.

Bartender, singing, pretty well, actually, but then he probably is sober:

"Then I saw her face,

"Now I'm gonna leave her,

"Not a chance

"That I'll stick around…"

Somebody else yells, "There is a bathroom on the right." Bad Moon boos, and the game disintegrates.

Lara staggers back to her suite and falls onto the bed fully clothed.

She remembers nothing.

"I left my brains down in Africa…"

In what was probably the next morning, she awoke to the ringing of the brick. It was Randall. She told him she was busy but would call back as soon as she was un-busy. The aspirin and the Folgers and the shower did their best, which was none too good. She called back.

"Where the hell have you been?" he asked.

"In jail."

"Oh, come on. You are shitting me."

"No, do you want me to tell you the whole story?"

He did, and she did—tell him in graphic detail.

"Oh Lara, I am so sorry I put you into this situation. Get the next plane home and send me a bill for everything you spent. This really has gotten out of control. I am calling off the whole site visit thing. It isn't worth it."

"But that is just the point, Randall, it is worth it because something really rotten is going on here, and we should get to the bottom of it."

"Lara, you understand that I am a POLITICAL appointee? I answer to multiple masters besides the president who put me here. I am getting heat, lots of it, from the congressional side that funds our budget every year. I have been told in no uncertain terms to back off, and that is just what I am doing. Come home."

"You are chickening out?"

"Yup, that is exactly what I am doing. I am not about to risk the existence of this agency to slap the hand of a little Cultural Center in Nowheresville."

She hung up without revealing her intentions.

She didn't know what her intentions were.

AFTER THE DISTRESSING CALL FROM RANDALL AND STILL feeling fuzzy from the alcohol lingering in her system, Lara decided to take a walk around town. No more forest running. Running would make her throw up anyway.

The town was not what you would call "walkable." Two blocks this way, and dead-end into a field. Go back and cross the highway, two blocks that way and then the slope of the rounded hill with cattle on it. Then it was return to the highway, walk to the next street, and repeat the process. Try not to get run over by a truck. The town was only a few blocks long. Not much to see.

Dysfunctional vehicles adorned most yards. There was logging equipment, much of it antique even to her unschooled eye, and lots of badges of poverty. One house stood out for its assembly of junk, but here Lara's artistic eye perceived order among the chaos. Her fuzzy mind's mind (it was hungover, too) remembered the "crazy lady" she had been advised to look up.

She made her way through the detritus to the front door and called, "Anybody home?"

The lady was old all right, but not feeble and definitely not senile. She invited Lara in. What ensued was one of the most literate and artistically insightful conversations Lara had ever had. The lady could give Stoney a run for her money in the cross-examination department. She bombarded Lara with a litany of mostly unanswerable questions:

"How do you define 'beautiful'?"

"You know, don't you, that the word history means 'to ask'?"

"In the end, to whom are we obligated to account?"

"Do you think the purpose of art is to embrace life's significant mistakes?"

"Is our survival conditioned on sacrifice?"

"Is struggle worthwhile in and of itself?"

"Do you think that all things on earth are animated with a life spirit?"

"Can a person be both innocent and virtuous?"

"Language fails us, but then love takes over. Do you believe that?"

"Do we construct cages that keep us from being free?"

"What does it mean to be 'civilized'?"

"Do we really want to see ourselves as we actually are?"

"What is art without risk?"

"Without mystery, can there be art?"

Lara sputtered and rambled. These were hard questions, impossible really, and she was in far from top form. But as the hours went by, she regained some focus, and realized that this lady was crazy all right—crazy smart. And gradually, the cup of tea helped, Lara turned the conversation to the lady herself—her name was Maud—and began asking questions of her own, like what had her life been? Why was she here?

Maud ducked the most personal questions, but she responded that she was here because art was here, and nobody was paying any attention.

"What kind of art?"

"It profits no one just to talk about art. We have proved that for the last two hours. Let me show you," Maud said, and she got up from her chair, showing no sign of aged knees or back, and held out her hand to Lara.

"These are rubbings from petroglyphs. The originals were inundated by a dam the Feds built near here. Another example of the ongoing disrespect shown to the genius of this continent's natives. These were made by a lady who is now dead. She entrusted them to me, and I have yet to discover a suitable home, but I will be damned if that Williams lady is going to get them."

"They are beautiful," said Lara.

"Beauty that is didactic. It is self-educated and self-explanatory."

"Look, now at these baskets. These are made from grasses and bark and vegetable dyes, and they are woven tight enough to hold water. 'Civilized' folks call this folk art—useful items made beautiful. But that is an uncivilized definition. These baskets represent art that is integral to their lives. They wouldn't even call it art any more than you would have to introduce yourself to yourself. It is simply and beautifully who they are, and as long as these wonders exist it gives us a glimpse of who they were."

Other shelves in Maud's basement held carvings, and what westerners call papoose carriers, and war clubs. "Yes, they were warlike, when they had to be. Humans fight. No getting around that. But these folks were just trying to stay alive. They were using what they needed and living in peace with nature."

"You said you would not let the Williams lady get her hands on these things. What did you mean?"

"She is a perfidious witness to the world of art; a really nasty piece of news. Money is what she is about, and money is about the least artistic thing I can think of. For her, nothing has value, and everything has a price. If she could, she would buy the ocean."

Lara loved this lady. She had known her for a couple of hours, and yet she felt like an acquaintance of a lifetime; an intimate friend; one soul dwelling in two bodies.

Maud continued: "She knows about the wonders I am showing you and she wants them, not to treasure and preserve, but to sell. She is a human smudge with a mind full of slugs. I can think of no one I more loathe. In my view, she luxuriates in her narcissistic personality disorder."

Lara had to laugh. Maud looked at her, smiled, then broke into a body-shaking cackle: heh, heh, heh, heh.

Maud said, "Let me tell you a story; a true story: The government was going to build an airport east of Glacier National Park in Montana, and they condemned the land only to change their mind, so the land reverted to the Indians. Chief Earl Old Person went to DC for the repatriation ceremony with Interior Secretary James Watt—a real low-voltage character, heh, heh, heh , heh. Earl Old Person took a beautifully beaded belt and gave it to Watt, saying: 'It is with great pleasure that I give you beads for your land.'"

Lara laughed again, and they embraced.

CHAPTER 15

The willfully deaf will never hear the music.

———◆———

S toney arrived for dinner in a skirt so short she could strut while sitting down. It was all Juan could do to keep from skipping dinner and going right to dessert.

They fell into each other's eyes.

This was high school on steroids.

They had food and then got right with the program.

Breathtaking.

Someday they would have to stop and get to know each other, but right now there wasn't time for that.

Meanwhile, Lara had decided that while Randall told her to come home, she could do a few more things first. One of them was to go back to the Cultural Center and pull out some of the artworks that Josh Bendix could not identify. She knew that there was significant traffic in both stolen and fake art purporting to be by important artists whose real works regularly sold for seven figures or more. Most of the ones Josh didn't recognize were of Russian origin. She took one purportedly by Kandinsky and hauled it up to the gallery where what was supposedly a legitimate Kandinsky hung. She leaned it against the wall, retreated to a bench, and sat staring at the two pieces.

Then she got up, stepped closer, and looked carefully, quadrant by quadrant, taking in all of the details. She tried to remember what her lover Michael had told her about authentication. In the end, she gave up because she just couldn't tell. What she did know was that there were certain badges of fraud that hung over fake pieces like a renegade fart. One of those was if a market had been made in sales of that artist's work by a single "art advisor."

Sometimes such a person would create fake sales—essentially selling to himself using strawmen, fake corporations, and the like. So if the identities of the buyer and seller were not transparent, that required caution. But then, wealthy and sophisticated collectors often did not want their identities known.

Manipulating the market in stocks is a crime. In artwork, not so much.

If the work had been appraised, the credentials of the appraiser must be checked for their bona fides. Windshield appraisals had been around in the housing market for decades. An art appraiser could weave a web of bullshit about a painting that would sound good and be completely devoid of substance.

Provenance is the history of an artwork. It starts with who created it and then traces its life through purchases, what was paid, where it has been displayed, and so forth. It is akin to the chain of custody of a piece of evidence. If there are holes in the narrative, look out. If a work suddenly just shows up, it is probably a fake.

Invoices can be faked. Money can be laundered by reporting exorbitant sale prices that do not reflect the market for a given work of art. The stock market has multiple levels of accountability, and it is still controlled by the big investors like insurance companies and hedge funds. The art market isn't supervised, period.

Sales for cash. That is a biggie. Drug money and other ill-gotten gains can come out smelling squeaky clean if the money has been traded for a work of art. Often these large sums are transferred in denominations of just under $10,000. Banks don't have to report those transactions. But if the money goes from a non-bank, say a museum, directly to the seller…Hmmmm.

⬩——◆——⬩

SHE HAULED JUAN OUT OF BED BY CALLING STONEY'S number enough times that she finally answered.

"Juan, get your clothes on and come up to the Cultural Center. I am supposed to be leaving. We have got a lot to do before I go and leave you to your own devices. And by the way, your devices seem to be getting quite a workout of late."

He groaned and he bitched but said he would be "up in an hour." Ha.

⬩——◆——⬩

LARA THEN CHATTED FOR A WHILE WITH LESTER AND Bradley, the two US marshals who had been looking after the place. It seemed that the logger-guards disappeared when Lara was in jail but reappeared when she got out. Hmm. Lester had determined that the booted ones worked for Williams Lumber, and they were quite open about their dedication to their employer. It sounded like a cult or a paramilitary organization, not a company purveying goods for commerce, but maybe it was both. Hmm.

Juan showed up looking happily bedraggled.

"Please get the blood back up to your brain and go through the purchases of art that show up in the books."

"Okay." He got to work with Lara looking over his shoulder.

"Can you tell where the purchase money comes from?"

"It just says donations in the notes. Doesn't say from whom."

"Does it show how much money has been 'donated' by Williams Lumber to the Cultural Center?"

"There should be letters acknowledging gifts. Companies can donate up to 5 percent of their pre-tax profits and get a deduction on their taxes, but I can't find any such records," said Juan.

Hmmm.

Lara had a dilemma. She needed to get back before Judge Carver and get him to order Piper Williams to show up for a deposition. To do this she had to get the US attorney back on the job, and figure out how she could speak for the NEA when she had been ordered to stand down.

She called George Graham.

"First, thank you for hiring me a lawyer. She is a real piece of work and was very effective. I will reimburse you, by the way. I don't think I could have endured another day in jail."

"You are welcome, but let's pause here, and recount the multiple lessons you have learned from this experience."

"Like what?"

"Like not running by yourself in a strange forest; driving and not paying attention to where you are and where you are going; not pissing off the local authorities; not disobeying those who sent you there. Any of those lessons ring true?"

"Come on George. You are the one who told me I have a nose that smells inconsistencies. You said I would make a fine investigator."

"I meant that in the abstract. I did not endorse your goading folks into trying to kill you. If you got yourself killed, I would hate you forever."

"That's sweet."

"I am afraid to ask why you are calling," he said, resigned that Lara would be Lara.

"I need you to get the US attorney to ask the judge to issue a subpoena, or whatever you call it, to make Piper Williams sit for a deposition. She is the only one who can tell us just what has been happening at the Cultural Center."

"Why aren't you asking your boss at the NEA to do that?"

"He is a chicken."

"Okay, I get it, the politicos have come down on him to cease and desist, and he has caved. Am I right?"

She reluctantly mumbled assent.

"Damnit Lara, we have done this dance before, and it nearly got you killed, and it did get me shot. You are a knucklehead."

"There is something really, really smelly going on out here, George, and nobody is going to do anything about it unless you help me."

"Do I hear you saying that you are going to do whatever you are going to do, regardless of whether I help you?"

"Maybe."

"You really piss me off, Lara."

"I have heard that before."

After Lara hung up, she thought to herself: I was the main contact with the US attorney. Maybe if I call him, he will lay a deposition notice on Piper Williams without calling Washington. Then she thought, if Piper is noticed for a deposition, the same political pressure will come welling up to squash or quash or whatever the term is when someone doesn't want to be deposed. No, I need the judge to call her in to his courtroom and make her answer.

This was too dicey, not to mention far beyond her authority, to do over the phone so she got in her rental car and drove to Eugene, where she could make her case in person. She consulted the directory in the lobby, found the US attorney's office, and walked in without an appointment. She told the receptionist that she had urgent business with her boss and sat down to wait. As she was sitting, rehearsing her request, who should stroll out of the back office, file in his hand but THE SEXY-SINGER GUY WITH THE DELIGHTFUL TUSH FROM THE CLEAN, PRESENTABLE DIVE. Holy shit.

They locked eyes, each with the unarticulated question: "What are you doing here?"

He, being the less dumbfounded, said: "You are the lady who was in the bar down in Roseburg for a while."

Lara, trying not to drool, said: "And you are the singer. What are you doing here?"

He: "I work here. I am an assistant US attorney. I go down to Roseburg a couple of times a month to sing and play. It is easier to do it out of town where I won't run into people from my day job."

At that point the receptionist announced that the US attorney would see Lara now. The singer/lawyer/sexpot smiled, nodded, and was gone. Lara reassembled her parts and followed the receptionist.

She told the US attorney of the extra money in the Cultural Center's accounts, the acquisition of art that could not be explained, and the suspicion that the Cultural Center was being used to launder money. She even suggested that the Cultural Center, or Piper Williams, was selling original art and replacing it with fakes. All of this, of course, was Lara's imagination working overtime, but she was used to flying by the seat of her pants. She was after all, as Randall had put it, the "Failure Queen."

She got the US attorney to draw up some affidavits about the necessity for immediate access to the information that only Piper Williams possessed, seasoned with some gratuitous references to the way Lara had been abused, threatened, and jailed, and, just to stick it to the Williamses, a couple of paragraphs saying that they, the Williamses, had exerted political pressure to try to prevent information about the center from coming to light. No judge likes to hear of or feel political pressure, least of all Judge Leighton Carver.

Lara fidgeted and worried, waiting for the hearing the judge ordered. Law courts were scary places, particularly after her recent visit to the cross-bar hotel. Fortunately, Judge Carver was, by nature, in a hurry. It was his job to get things resolved. The Motion to Compel Piper Williams to appear was met with a Motion to Quash by Piper's lawyers. The hearing took about five minutes. Judge Carver denied the Motion to Quash and set her deposition for the following Monday at 10 a.m. in his courtroom in Eugene. He would be available should any issues arise during the deposition that required his attention. Lara liked this judge. His courtroom was a friendly place.

Lara now had the weekend to hide. She knew she was in danger. She couldn't just walk the streets of the popedom. Salish was so small that she would be spotted in a heartbeat, and Roseburg was enemy territory. What to do.

She called her new best friend Maud. Of course, she could stay there. Maud knew she was known as the "crazy lady" and no one would be sniffing around her "junk-filled front yard." Lara stashed her car in Maud's garage (they had to move a bunch of stuff to get it in there), she turned off her phone, and they hunkered down for a nice, philosophical weekend. Lara told her about her associate, Wil Porter, who had copied an icon that was now permanently installed in Ukraine's highest and most revered church. That led to a discussion of what is real and what is a gimmick or a reflection; and the unanswerable questions continued as they progressed from tea to gin. A thoroughly delightful respite.

CHAPTER 16

The tongue consists of seven untrainable muscles.

The papacy was being fucked with.

Bill Williams had called his senators, but they told him that they didn't have any sway over a federal judge, and he was better off getting some first-class legal help. That response did not please the pope. He had first-class legal help, and so far they had been clobbered. But he was a realist, and so that is why he and Piper were sitting in his living room at the Victorian mansion talking to his first-class legal help. The advice Piper was getting was: "Listen to the question, answer only that question and stop. If you don't understand the question, ask for clarification. If I object, don't say anything until I either tell you not to answer, or to go ahead."

"What if I don't want to answer the question?" That was Piper.

"A subpoena isn't a party invitation you can decline. The deposition is scheduled for the judge's courtroom specifically so he can be on hand to resolve any disputes. While we lawyers may misbehave and bend the deposition rules if the depo is in one of our offices, if the judge is right behind a door in his chambers, we are all on our best behavior."

"But I am not going to answer any question I find inappropriate or annoying," Piper said.

"Mrs. Williams, that is not the applicable standard. The scope of a discovery deposition such as this one is very broad, and the judge will give the inquiring attorney lots of leeway to find out what you know."

"This is bullshit!" she stood up to go. Bill put his hand on her arm. He stood with her and talked quietly in her ear. She sat.

"What," she said, "will they do if I exercise my right against self-incrimination—taking the Fifth, I think they call it."

The first-class lawyer (his name was Haskins) was surprised by this. "Why in the world would you do that? The Fifth Amendment is for criminal proceedings. This is just about the doings of an art center. You can't seriously want to suggest you are involved in criminal behavior?"

"I'll do what I have to do," she said, and that ended the preparation session.

Her first-class lawyer knew he had a first-class problem on his hands. An uncontrollable client is a lawyer's worst nightmare.

LARA HAD CALLED STONEY OVER THE WEEKEND AND asked her to attend Piper Williams's deposition. Stoney was delighted, had a few pejoratives to describe Piper, and told Lara she would give her a ride. That was good with Lara since her car was known to the local malefactors. Stoney would pick her up.

Varoom, Varoom, VAROOM! That was Stoney's calling card on Monday morning. Lara peeked out to see her on a motorcycle motioning for Lara to come out. Stoney handed her a leather jacket and helmet and said, "Hop on." Lara loved this sort of thing—a little unscheduled danger and excitement. She was an adrenaline junky. She donned the helmet, zipped up the jacket, hopped on with one arm around Stoney's middle, and with a circular swing of the other yelled: "Let her rip."

Rip, they did.

Yelling over the roar of the Harley's engine and the wind whistling past her face shield, Stoney said she knew some back roads that would get them there just as fast, and if any assholes were looking for them they wouldn't see squat.

Stoney parked her bike in the courthouse lot, they shed their leather gear and became as presentable as fifty minutes of 70 mph wind could allow, and made their way to Judge Carver's courtroom. Lara kept a keen eye out for the lawyer/singer/eye candy guy whose name she still didn't know, but no luck and no heart palpitations.

A bunch of lawyers were milling around, a court reporter was setting up her machine, there was a vacuum pot of coffee on a side table, and a US marshal was there just in case anybody needed to be shot. Who wasn't there was the deponent: Piper Williams. The two counsel tables, usually on opposite sides of the courtroom had been pushed together. At a few minutes before ten, lawyers started unpacking their briefcases, getting yellow pads and pens out, and sharpening their wits for the festivities.

They waited.

At ten past ten, the US attorney said: "On the record, please."

The court reporter, hands poised over her stenotype machine (a little gizmo with a keyboard that makes shorthand squiggles on a narrow, continuous feed stack of paper) waited.

US attorney: "This is the time set for the deposition of Piper Williams in the case entitled *United States of America v. Left Coast Cultural Center,*" he read the case number. "In accordance with the order of the Honorable Judge Leighton Carver, the deponent was to report here, at the United States Courthouse, Eugene, Oregon, to give testimony, under oath, beginning at ten o'clock a.m. this date. It is now (he looked at the wall clock) ten fourteen, and the deponent has not shown up. Mr. Haskins (Piper's first-class attorney), do you know where she is?"

Haskins: "She was served with the order along with a Subpoena Duces Tecum (means, bring along all the specified papers and documents). I have reviewed her testimony with her, and both she and her husband assured me they knew the seriousness of this matter and would be here."

US attorney: "We will wait a few minutes more. Is there any number you can call?"

Haskins: "I don't have a car phone or other mobile number, no."

US attorney: "Well, if she isn't here by half-past, I will ask the judge…"

The courtroom door opened and in strolled—no, *processed*—Piper, followed by Bill Williams and the ubiquitous butler. She was dressed to the nines—even had a Greta Garbo hat with a turned down brim and a pheasant feather. She stood near the empty chair at the head of the table. The men around the table, lawyers all, stood, even the US attorney; they couldn't help it. Haskins moved around to hold her chair. She sat.

She had already won round one.

US attorney: "The witness will be sworn." The court reporter administered the oath: "You do solemnly swear that the testimony you are about to give is the truth, the whole truth, and nothing but the truth, so help you, God."

Piper nodded.

US attorney: "Ms. Williams, you have to speak audibly for the record."

Ms. Williams: "Okay."

US attorney: "I mean, you have to swear to the oath you have been given out loud."

Williams: "Okay."

US attorney: "Madam court reporter, would you please administer the oath again?"

She did, but Piper did not raise her right hand as instructed and at the end, again said: "Okay."

US attorney: "I am not satisfied that the witness has agreed to the oath…"

Haskins: "I object. She has assented twice."

US attorney: "We have agreed that all objections are preserved for later ruling if there is a dispute."

Then three or four lawyers started talking at once, and the court reporter screamed: "One person at a time—I can only take down one person at a time."

Things quieted down.

Piper sat with a beatific smile.

US attorney: "State your full name for the record, please."

Williams: "Piper Marsh Williams."

US attorney: "You understand that the oath you have taken here is the same as if you were a witness in a trial, and the penalty for a false answer, that is for perjury, is the same."

Haskins: "Objection. Trying to intimidate the witness."

US attorney: "All objections are reserved. That is our agreement. If you keep interjecting, we will be here for a very long time."

Then multiple lawyers started talking; the court reporter started screaming.

Order gradually returned.

US attorney: "You were served with a subpoena to bring documents relating to the business affairs of the Left Coast Cultural Center. Did you bring those documents?"

Williams: "No."

US attorney: "Why not?"

Williams: "Any documents are the property of the Cultural Center. They are not mine personally."

US attorney: "Do you hold an official title with the Cultural Center?"

Williams: "I do."

US attorney: "What is it?"

Williams: "Chair of the Board of Trustees."

US attorney: "As Chair of the Trustees, you could order someone to bring the requested documents, couldn't you?"

Williams: "I suppose so, but there is no one there who could do that."

It went on like this for another forty-five minutes, the US attorney getting absolutely no useful information from Piper.

They took a break.

Stoney introduced herself to the US attorney, said she was the lawyer for the representative of the National Endowment for the Arts, and asked if she could lay a few questions on the reluctant but increasingly smug Piper. He didn't see why not; he was getting nowhere.

They reconvened. Haskins objected to Stoney inquiring, but since he had reserved objections, and since he wanted to obstruct, but not enough that someone would call the judge in to kick ass, he relented.

Ms. Stone: "Do you know who killed Linda McKenzie?"

Williams: "Why would I know that?"

Stone: "Answer the question."

Williams: "No."

Stone: "Isn't it true that Williams Lumber has paid in over $550,000 to the Cultural Center in the last fiscal year?"

Williams: "I don't know."

Stone: "As head of the trustees, isn't it your job to ensure fiscal responsibility of your nonprofit organization?"

Williams: "We have professionals who do that."

Stone: "You didn't answer my question. It is your responsibility, isn't it?"

Williams: "Don't you dare yell at me, young lady."

Stone: "You'll know if I am yelling. Answer the question."

Williams: "I don't have to take this."

Stone: "Isn't it true that Williams Lumber is laundering money it has received from trees stolen from Forest Service or BLM land through the Cultural Center?"

Williams: "How dare you…"

All hell breaks loose. Attracted by the hullabaloo, Judge Carver opens the door from his chambers and strolls in. He is wearing half-glasses, suspenders, and a bowtie. And shoes, socks, and trousers, of course.

Judge: "Pretty noisy in here. What is going on?"

Everyone talking at once.

Judge: "One at a time, please. Mr. US Attorney?"

US attorney: (Nodding to the court reporter to continue the record) "Judge, we have been here for an hour and one half and have not gotten one straight answer. She was served with a subpoena, she is the chair of the trustees, and she claims there is no one to provide the requested documents. We are getting stonewalled."

Everyone talking at once.

Judge: "Which one of you represents her?"

Haskins: "I do, Your Honor."

Judge: "How long will it take to get the requested documents?"

Haskins: "I don't know."

Judge: "Shouldn't be that hard if the records have been kept as they should be. Here is my order (nodding to the court reporter): You and your client will appear here with all requested documents one week from today to continue this deposition."

With that he pivoted around, returned to his chambers, and closed the door.

The ride back on Stoney's Harley was just as fast but not as much fun since the deposition had been a bust. Two things were clear to Lara. First, the week until Piper's next deposition would give them plenty of time to cook the books or destroy whatever evidence might be incriminating; and second, there was no way Lara could justify hanging around any longer, particularly since the word of her frolic and detour in pursuing the lawsuit on her own initiative would surely filter back to Randall, and he would be mightily honked off. She needed to get back to DC for a sit-down. She hated to do it because that damn sexy-singer-lawyer-stud-muffin had invaded her mind.

She got a plane ticket, drove to Portland, returned her rental car, and decided that rather than make an appointment, she would just show up at Randall's office and lay some razzmatazz on him about why he should care about this case long enough to see it through.

Why did she care?

Because, she told herself, I have taken on a project and when I do, it is incumbent on me to see it through to the end. Then her mind's mind, which she thought was in league with the smear of Catholic guilt the church had spread on her, piped up and told her that she was guilty of the sin of pride—one of the seven deadlies—and that she should put her faith in a higher power and stop trying to manage her chaotic life herself.

Fat chance. I signed up for this job, and I will finish it. Her mind's mind responded with a rude sound.

———◆———

THE PLANE WAS A RED-EYE THAT GOT TO DULLES AT 7 a.m. She took a shuttle downtown, grabbed some breakfast in the spacious lobby of the Old Post Office Building on Pennsylvania Avenue about halfway between the White House and the Capitol, and marveled at the magnificence of the building and how poorly it worked as an office. The lobby/atrium was seven stories high. The upper floor hallways had banisters overlooking the shops and restaurants below, the noise from which produced a cacophony like the inside of a drum, making conversation in the hallways nearly impossible. Still, it was a great building that housed the offices of the National Endowment for the Arts. It would be a shame if it ever became, I don't know…a hotel?

The chairman's office was in one of the four corners of the seventh floor. She had been there multiple times but had always had an appointment. To get upstairs, one had to check in with the building guards or have a credential. The guards would call up to whoever the visitor was seeing, and that person would send down an escort. This was partly a matter of security, and partly to keep nosy and supremely annoying journalists from the *Washington Times* from roaming the halls looking for smut.

Lara had neither a credential nor an appointment.

No problem. She gave the guard the name of a friend who worked in Folk Arts, greeted an escort that got her as far as the elevators, popped up to the seventh floor, and strolled into the chairman's office as if she owned the place. Randall's assistant said she would "see if he was in." Lara marched in right behind her and said: "Randall, my friend, you have got a problem, and we have to talk." She nodded to Randall's assistant to dismiss her. "Close the door, please."

Randall sat at his antique desk, mouth agape as Lara, talking a mile a minute, took one of the guest chairs and let fly with a blizzard of fact and speculation, the sum total of which was that money the NEA had given was being used in a criminal enterprise and they had better get the mess cleaned up before the newspapers got it and he got himself reamed a new one.

It worked. She had so snowed him that he forgot to get mad and ream her a new one.

LARA RECOUNTED THAT THE CULTURAL CENTER HAD lousy books that failed to disclose a traceable path from donations to their general fund. They had too much money, and the budget they submitted to the NEA to get the advancement grant was probably fraudulent. They had no leadership at this point, so the whole purpose of advancement to a higher level of efficiency and success was a joke. Piper Williams, if not a criminal, was the least cooperative rectum-ette Lara had ever encountered, and the prospect of working with her to salvage the grant was truly frightening.

Beyond that, the office computers at the center were missing, and Piper would be hard at work sanitizing the numbers before her deposition next week. Only by decisive action on his—that is, Randall's—part, could the NEA recover its money, expose the malfeasance, and wax heroic.

Stunned as he was, Randall had the good sense to pick up the phone and invite his general counsel, the historically named Peter French, to join them. This meant that Lara got to spin her tale again, this time suggesting that they needed investigative help big time, and she would be glad to contact her friend George Graham at the FBI. Randall and Peter were way out of their depth. Good judgment comes from experience, and experience often comes from bad judgment. They told Lara to go ahead.

As she got up to leave, Randall said: "Give me back my phone."

"Glad to get it out of my purse. It weighs a ton."

CHAPTER 17

Thoughts are like dinner guests; listen and decide whether you want to invite them back.

L ara didn't think she could just talk her way in to see George Graham. They indeed had a bond from their time in Russia when she had the famous Icon. They were close, like father and daughter. But he was a senior special agent, and she couldn't pull a Randall and just barge in. So she called. He was delighted that she was "out of harm's way" and agreed to lunch. He would order up sandwiches, and they could eat in his conference room. She promised full disclosure of her latest adventures.

She was dead on her feet after the red-eye, but there wasn't time to go out to her house, an hour-plus drive west in Flint Hill, Virginia. She had a phone card, so she went to the East Building of the National Gallery, that splendid I.M. Pei structure, found a bank of pay phones, and called Juan.

Stoney had filled him in on the fruitless deposition of Piper, and he was copying as many of the financial records as he could in anticipation that Piper would be in to muck with them. The other bit of news from Salish was that a US Forest Service guy named John Rawlings was trying to find her. He had left his number, which Lara copied down. Juan thought his work there in Salish might just take a couple of months more. The pleasures of Stoney compelled it.

When Lara reached John Rawlings, he told her that he had personally inspected multiple stands of Forest Service and Bureau of Land Management timber, and had cruisers look at a bunch more. He had found the place where timber rustlers had swiped some old growth trees—the place Lara paused when she was fleeing her chasers. But, the news was that the patch Lara found was the only theft they could identify. If there was any big-time rustling going on, it wasn't around here.

"So why did you want to talk to me if there isn't a timber theft issue," asked Lara.

"Well, that's the thing. You know that the parcels are checkerboarded around here, this section owned by BLM, the state, or the Forest Service, and that one in private hands?"

"No, I didn't know that. So what?"

"The guys that were cruising noticed some bright green patches on the private land. All those private sections are Williams Lumber or Bill Williams's personally."

"Help me out, John, I am not following."

"Well, I told the wife about it, and she thinks it is marijuana. She said I should call you."

Oops.

THE FIRST THING LARA TOLD GEORGE GRAHAM WAS about the suspected marijuana. If Linda McKenzie was prone to take long walks in the woods, and if she stumbled across the marijuana (which notwithstanding its incumbency on many street corners in Oregon, was a Schedule I narcotic in the eyes of the federal government) she could have been abducted and killed by the growers. Putting her in a coffin and dumping her in the cemetery would be their way of warning off any curious or stupid people who might want to wander by their operation.

He didn't react. Just listened.

Next she described the deposition of Piper Williams, the most uncooperative of witnesses. He shrugged that off.

Most witnesses he encountered were reluctant.

Next she recounted the lack of meaningful records kept by the Cultural Center.

So what?

Well—she was getting a little pissed at his nonchalance; she had, after all, been chased by car and foot—it was federal money and her charge was to account for it, and she couldn't do that.

Some assignments don't pan out. Agents run up blind alleys all the time in the investigation business. That's what he said.

Well, how would he explain that the Cultural Center had too much money?

Not enough money is usually what gets our attention.

"Goddammit, George, I am trying to get you interested, and all you are doing is jerking my chain."

"Sweetie, Sweetie, I am messin' with you because you are so serious and sincere. You got a bone between your teeth and you aren't going to let go of it, but what you have is just speculation, and no hard evidence of anything other than incompetence. Pull the grant from this outfit, make a claim for return of the money in that lawsuit, and be done with it."

"What about the lady that was killed? You guys care about murders, don't you?" Lara was smoked, and it wasn't weed. He was toying with her.

He grabbed her in a big bear hug. She wiggled for a while, then relaxed. She looked up at his big, brown, bald head, and bigger smile and gave a sheepish little grin back. He had her number.

"I think I know why you do this, Lara. You can't be comfortable with being comfortable. You need a challenge; something to grow by. And, you are trying to outrun the God you have forsaken, and you are terrified that faith might overtake you and gobble you up."

She loved this man, but the fact that he had her number fried her butt.

WHEN LARA LEFT GRAHAM'S OFFICE, SHE WONDERED about Linda McKenzie. She still had her dad's number at the college in Ashland. She called. Did Linda like to walk in the woods? Absolutely, she would go off by herself for hours at a time. She had a marvelous sense of direction. Always could find her way right back to her car. Never got lost.

PIPER WILLIAMS HAD ENJOYED HER DEPOSITION. NOT many folks do, but she had been successful in giving up almost no information. She liked sparring with lawyers, most of whom, in her estimation, were supercilious twits. Now she had a week to sanitize the center's records and concoct some financial-appearing detritus that would disclose no information. Her choice here was between criminality and incompetence. Since there weren't a lot of others to blame, incompetence it would have to be. She could play that role, too.

First, though, she had to have a Come to Jesus, or maybe Moses or Allah, understanding with Sam. Sam was probably not really his name any more than Sergei Ashkenazy was.

She called a number. An accented voice answered by repeating the last four digits she had dialed.

She asked for Sam.

"No Sam here" was the reply. Click.

She waited, five, fifteen, thirty minutes, and her phone rang.

"Hello."

"No names, please, yes?"

"Just a heads-up for you. I have both state and federal snoops looking around here, and they might be contacting you."

"What is this 'heads-up?' This 'snoops?' You don't know English, yes?"

"You understand perfectly well, and you are warned." This time it was her turn to click.

Piper wasn't much worried about Sam. He was savvy and with his work as an art advisor and appraiser, much of which was a matter of opinion, he didn't pose a significant threat. But there was another weak link, and about him, she had substantial concern.

WHEN PIPER, WITH HER BUTLER ACTING AS CHAUFFEUR, arrived at the Left Coast Cultural Center in her block-long

Mercedes 600, she greeted Lester and Bradley as if they were long-lost cousins. Except, she really didn't pull it off, and when she extended her gloved hand, wrist slightly elevated, they shook it rather than kissed it.

The logger-guards, who had unslouched from their chairs and were standing at a kind of ragged attention the minute they saw the Mercedes arriving, might as well not have been there. She ignored them entirely.

To the marshals, she said: "I am surprised you gentlemen (on her tongue the word became a pejorative) are still here. The court has ordered me to retrieve records, and that is what I am going to do. I expect you will behave yourselves."

With that, she ascended the steps, produced a key, opened the front door (it was unlocked already, but she was into symbols of power), and proceeded to the administrative offices, where Juan Oropallo was trying to recover from a night of sexual ecstasy.

Upon seeing her, trailed by her butler/chauffeur, he leaped out of his chair and blushed full flower as if he had been caught with his hand in the till or, in this case, in his trousers.

"Did you know, young man, that humans are the only animal that blushes, and a blush cannot be faked? You must have been doing something naughty."

His thoughts had definitely been naughty. Struggling to unblush, he figured out who this was and introduced himself.

"Oropallo? Does that mean a gold chicken in Spanish?" she asked.

"No, Ma'am" was all he could manage in reply.

"Well, sit back down, Mister Gold Chicken, and I will be about my business here, and you can watch and report to the nice judge if you want." To her butler, who apparently did not have a name, she nodded and said: "Get the boxes and get busy."

He retrieved a bundle of flattened bankers boxes from the trunk (he probably called it a boot) of the Mercedes, assembled them, and began systematically cleaning out the files of the Cultural Center.

Piper sat and watched, making no attempt to talk to the gold chicken, and when the butler had hauled the last box out to the car, she rose, and without a word, processed back to the car, nodded to her butler/chauffeur as he held the back door, and was gone.

JUAN CALLED HIS SUPERVISOR AT THE ATTORNEY GENeral's office and then Lara to report the clean-out. His supervisor told him to call Jim Stetson and see what, if anything, he wanted to do about it. She also wondered how much longer Juan intended to stay in the Roseburg area.

To Lara, Juan said: "Mrs. Williams and a guy with big muscles arrived in a mammoth car and hauled away all of the records of the Cultural Center."

"What did she say she was doing?"

"To me, nothing. She treated me like a peasant. She told Lester and Bradley that the judge ordered her to take them."

"Well," said Lara, "the judge did order her to produce records at the continuance of her deposition, so I guess there isn't much we can do about it."

"Here is what I think about the whole deal," said Juan:

"She marched in here like she owned it.

"She scooped up the papers, that's no-shit.

"She gave me a sneer,

"Said I wasn't her peer.

"She's a twit with a zit in her arm-pit."

"Juan, I will not dignify your assault on our language as poetry. The meter and the structure, the sound and the content compel multiple explorations because the music of poetry is all the best words in the best order. What you do with your limericks, however, strikes me as the lowest form of drivel, and I know you 'only do it to annoy because you know it teases.' When are you going home?"

"Never, if I can help it."

CHAPTER 18

Stupid doesn't have a mind of its own. That's the problem.

———◆———

Back in Randall's high-ceilinged corner office in the Old Post Office Building on Pennsylvania Avenue— what a treasure this building is; the government was so wise to use it for federal offices; it would be a shame if it ever fell into private hands—Lara was trying to persuade Randall to hire an expert in Russian avant-garde painting to examine the works at the Left Coast Cultural Center.

"Why would I do this? If I get called up before the Congress and Representative John Dingle is staring over his half glasses at me, do I say I did it because a museum director named Lara Cole told me to?"

"What am I—chopped liver?"

"Aren't you the one who caused an international incident over that icon?"

"That is entirely unfair, Randall. You know I didn't want it, argued against it, and did everything I could to return it. And anyway, you owe me because you were of absolutely no help in that disaster."

"Give me the talking points. Tell me what I say if I have to justify spending federal money to evaluate the holdings of one of our grantees. Keep in mind, please, that the bigwigs behind this center are wired in politically, and every time I touch it I get a shock."

"Point number one: $250,000 has been pledged and $125,000 disbursed to this outfit, and you have an obligation to see it is well and truly spent.

"Number two: you sent me out there to do just that, and I found the place a mess.

"Number three: that mess includes books that are indecipherable (and now probably completely cooked).

"Number four: all the leadership is fired or murdered.

"Number five: Piper Williams is the sole remaining trustee, and she stonewalled your lawyers in a deposition seeking information about the center.

"Number Six: Piper Williams is a scumbag and probably a criminal, and is, in my humble opinion, one of the most unpleasant humans on the planet."

"Nice list," he said. "I particularly like number six and would just love to see it attributed to me on the front page of the Washington Post."

"Come on, Randall, the other points on the list are persuasive. You have an obligation to be a good steward of the people's money—that is the single most credible answer you could give to any congressional inquiry."

"What you haven't answered, Lara, is what I say to Oregon senators Fred and Andy when their staffers call me and wonder why I have a hard-on for the poor little museum the Williamses love."

"OK, here is a solution. You have already hired me, and I have investigated, but made no report. Tell me that you will approve a bill from an appraiser/authenticator. I will find and hire one, and if it gets sticky you can blame me. I have broad shoulders."

He didn't say anything, but he sort of dropped his head, and she took it as a sign of surrender and hurried out of there.

———◆—◆———

THE DIRECTOR OF THE PORTLAND ART MUSEUM SAID HE had a Russian scholar on staff, and he would check if she knew enough about the avant-garde period to spot a fake. If she did, he would drive her down himself because he was curious about the Left Coast Cultural Center and wanted to check it out. He could absorb the cost in his budget as long as it didn't get into detailed reports, court testimony, and that kind of foolishness.

He called back half an hour later to report that Sonya had written her doctoral thesis on Russian modernists and was enthusiastic for this adventure. Would tomorrow be too soon? By car they could be there in a little under three hours.

———◆—◆———

THE CULTURAL CENTER, EVERY ASPECT OF WHICH WAS becoming increasingly creepy, engendered dread rather than enthusiasm in Lara, but she was happy to be back on the job—there was lots still to do.

She dialed up Jim Stetson, the Douglas County DA.

"What do you know about marijuana?"

"I haven't smoked any today; why do you ask?"

"I have reports from some timber cruisers and a Forest Service guy in Salish named John Rawlings that there are bright green patches on sections of forest land abutting BLM and Forest Service holdings. Rawlings said they were checkerboarded, whatever that means."

"It just means they are intermixed. Historically it has to do with a failed railroad project, the Homestead Act of 1862, and a bunch of other land swaps. Most of the private land around here belongs to Bill Williams or his company."

"Could you check it out?"

"Not much else on my plate right now. Give me the number of the Forest Service guy."

PIPER WILLIAMS DID NOT GO OUT MUCH. SHE HAD MOST everything she needed at home, home being a modest 6,000-square-foot castle with a full gym, swimming pool, and lots of rooms to decorate, redecorate, and relax in. The butler did the grocery shopping; the cook lived in. On her monthly trips to San Francisco, she ate out at suitable restaurants such as there weren't in Roseburg.

She was uneasy, though. She just didn't know how much Bill knew. She had made herself available for nookie and pillow talk although they "shared separate bedrooms." He was unconcerned about the Cultural Center. Whenever she brought it up, all he said was "how much more (money) do they need?" He was willing to give it, no questions asked. She wasn't even sure if he knew the place was essentially defunct. She could give a shit about whether it was or wasn't—defunct, that is—but defunctness would put a major crimp in her little sidelines, and she would miss that very much.

For one of her sidelines, she needed to have a face-to-face talk. Being driven out in the big Mercedes was fine if she wanted the vassals and peasants to have something to gossip about, but for this, she needed to be inconspicuous. Inconspicuous was not in her DNA.

We interrupt this program to bring you a commercial from the God of Abraham, the God of vengeance, the God that holds you over the fiery furnace, who abhors your sins and calls you to REPENT. Sins come in sevens: pride, lust, covetousness, anger, sloth, envy. Am I forgetting one? Covetousness is greed. Maybe they are the same, maybe not, but I bring you this message in the hope that you can forsake greed. You don't need it all. I, your God—look me in the eye here—no, don't, cause if you do you will perish. Just listen: if you have everything you could possibly want, why do you want more? It is a sickness. But what really twists my torso, is that I have given you all these riches and you are colossally ungrateful. Watch out, Lady, 'cause I'm talking to YOU. You are like that rotten King Nebuchadnezzar who didn't respect me. I am the one holding you by the scruff of the neck over the lake of burning brimstone. Your wickedness gives you weight like lead. You are like a loathsome insect, and the hoods of my vengeance abhor you. Beware the wrath to come. I am pissed off. Oh, and by the way, gluttony is the seventh deadly sin.

Back to your regularly scheduled program.

SHE GOT DRESSED, LOOKED IN THE MIRROR, AND EVEN SHE acknowledged that she looked like an REI commercial. The boots were new, not a scuff on them, the shirt still had fold marks, the pants had not seen a thorn or a clod of dirt. She looked expensive, not woodsy. Well, it would have to do. She wasn't about to go out and roll around in the dirt. No way.

She got the keys to her Rabbit. This Volkswagen had been hers when she was Piper Marsh, and she had kept it, in part to remind her where she had come from, not that she had the least bit of nostalgia for that shit-bird existence. It started right up, albeit with a big cloud of blue smoke, and she headed off. She had read somewhere that it was illegal to own a rabbit (a flesh and blood one) in Australia unless you were a magician. It made her smile. She wasn't a magician, but she knew lots of tricks.

JIM STETSON WAS IN THE LAW LIBRARY. HE HAD GRADU-ated from law school just about the time law books, the con-sistently bound tomes of cases, put together by a reporter for each judicial district, were being superseded by online electronic reporting. He hated it. What he liked about research was pulling down the book, reading the case he was after, and the one before and after it because the reporter sometimes bunched cases that had similar issues. He had backed into as many solutions as he had found straight on. Finding the "spotted cow," the case that was perfect on both the facts and the law that would blow the other side out of the water, was his greatest joy.

Right now, he was researching search and seizure. Every prosecutor knows about "the fruit of the poisonous tree." It had screwed up more prosecutions than a rancid, equivocating victim. Basically, the doctrine held that if a search was flawed by an invasion of privacy, or a false affidavit or any other deficiency that violated the accused's Fourth or Fifth Amendment rights, everything that followed on from that toxin would be excluded.

He had found a federal case out of Michigan, of first impression, which just means that the law books had not seen this issue resolved by a court before. A farmer was growing marijuana in a field shielded by trees, at the end of the road, that was described in very unjudicial language as in the "boondocks." The cops had gotten an anonymous tip, had piled into a small plane, and had made a pass over the field, first at 200 feet and then at 50. The farmer argued that his privacy had been invaded and thus the discovery of the marijuana was an unreasonable search and seizure in violation of his Fourth Amendment protections.

Privacy, said the court, protects people, not places. Outside of the home or other places society considers intimate, privacy depends on "a reasonable expectation," and nobody has such an expectation in an open field.

Pretty close, he thought. Yes, people go out into the forest to be alone, but that is different from locking yourself in your bedroom. If you are taking a dump behind a tree and a hiker comes along, your privacy has not been invaded. The forest is about as far from a home as one can get.

Awwright! Time to get a plane.

———————

The VW Rabbit pulled up at the end of a logging road. Bertie recognized it immediately. It was the same car she had in college. He had been in love with her from accounting class to this day, but seldom did she favor him with her charms. He was dumb, he knew he was dumb, but not so dumb that he didn't know when he was being used. Nonetheless, she bewitched him, and his powers of resistance were no match for her scent.

She stepped out. She was magnificent. She was pristine in her unrumpled clothes. She was irresistibly woman. She made his pants swell. He was lost from the get-go.

CHAPTER 19

I can hear you thinking.

B est for aerial reconnaissance is a high-wing, fixed-gear aircraft like a Cessna 172, a single-engine, relatively slow craft that is reliable, if noisy as hell, and can carry a pilot and observer. If the noise scares the growers into destroying their crop, so much to the good.

Stetson was fitted with Mickey Mouse headphones that let him talk to the pilot, and were supposed to cancel the engine noise, which they didn't. He had a digital camera with a long lens. It was morning—the best time for spotting the marijuana leaves when they were fresh and radiant. He told the state police pilot to try to keep the plane between the sun and the area they were looking at. Flying 500-800 feet above the treetops tightened his sphincters, but this was REALLY FUN!

Stetson could hardly wait to get back to town to print his pictures. This digital stuff was really great—no more waiting for film to be developed. They had located five places they thought were grow patches. All were near a stream, which made sense since marijuana needs lots of water. The pilot had a pretty good fix on the locations. This could turn into a big bust. Whoo-ee.

PIPER HAD SEEN THE PLANE FLYING AROUND, AND SHE knew exactly what it meant. She had to get these guys to work fast to get the crop harvested and then get lost. The smartest thing would have been for all of the workers to flee right now, but Piper, being Piper and totally disregarding anything she might have heard from a higher power, or even from her underdeveloped conscience, wasn't about to forgo the profits of a bumper crop.

She pulled Bertie aside, linked her arm around the back of his neck, pressed close to him, and told him to get his ass in gear and get those plants to market. He protested that the crop needed a couple more weeks. She said, "Now!"

Whether he appreciated that the plane was probably the law, or if he did, what he thought about it, mattered not in the least to Piper. She rubbed herself into him, flashed her eyelashes a bit, and gave him a kiss on the cheek. He would do as instructed; she had not a moment's doubt about that.

STETSON HAD AN AFFIDAVIT AND A SEARCH WARRANT ready an hour after landing. The affidavit had three pictures attached and incorporated along with an affirmation from the pilot of their location and Stetson's own testimony that the shape and bright green color of the plants, along with their remote and partially hidden location, all produced a reasonable belief that illegality was sprouting from the earth. A state circuit court judge signed the search warrant, and fifteen minutes later four vans carrying state police, Douglas County sheriff's deputies, and the county SWAT team were on their way. Piper passed them in her VW Rabbit as she was heading back to town. The jig was up and they would nab Bertie. Bad news, but something she hoped Bill could take care of. This would take some careful maneuvering. She probably should have played it safe and told Bertie to vamoose, but to give up all that profit…? Damn.

———◆———

BERTIE, EVEN WITH HIS HEAD FULL OF FUMES, KNEW HE was screwed the moment he saw the first van squirreling up behind his pickup. His workers, many of them undocumented, fled like real rabbits into the timber, hopefully never to be seen again. Bertie thought of running, but his pickup registration would give him away, and Bill had always been able to fix stuff like this in the past. Anyway, he was facing a dozen guys with body armor, helmets with face shields, and some very nasty looking weapons.

He raised his hands.

They cuffed Bertie in plastic ties, read him his rights, and tossed him in the luggage compartment of one of the vans as they searched the place. They counted over 8,750 plants in five plots. Under a tentlike structure they recovered more than a ton of partially processed weed and over $4,500 cash in a safe buried in the ground. There were also five rifles, a shotgun, and half a dozen handguns.

———◆———

CALIFORNIA HAD JUST PASSED PROPOSITION 215 THAT legalized medical marijuana. It was an open invitation for a skunk works such as this to grow illegally and sell legally. What a deal. Bertie had even heard that they had a whole town down there called Weed, although he didn't believe it.

He and his workers had constructed an ingenious still-like contraption with curly pipes and valves to extract the THC oils from the biomass. It would have warmed the heart of the most dedicated moonshiner. A kilogram of cannabis oil could bring as much as $30,000 where it wasn't legal (everywhere but California), but the proximity of legal markets to the south lessened the risk, and the profits would have been enormous.

———————

TRAP LABS LIKE THIS WERE NOT JUST ILLEGAL (MARI-juana in the eyes of the feds was a Schedule I narcotic like heroin and ecstasy), but they were prone to exploding and burning down the forest.

The plants would be destroyed with a tractor, where it could get to them, and by rototiller or hand tools or pesticides where the terrain was too rough. The authorities spent the better part of the day photographing, inventorying, and otherwise securing the site.

When they returned to the van where Bertie was being held, there was no Bertie.

———————

THE NIGHTLY NEWS AS FAR DISTANT AS DC TOLD OF THE spectacular weed bust out in the wilds of Ore-gone. Stetson was on the horn to Lara that night, still flying high, figuratively, about how much fun it was. He did mention that their one suspect had escaped by kicking open the back doors of the van where he was being held and walking away with his hands secured behind his back. No sweat, they would find him; they had his pickup. The press was all over it, calling it the biggest drug bust in Oregon's history, and he was the point man destined for immortality, or at least, re-election. Yee-haw.

———◆———

LARA HADN'T KNOWN WHO "BERTIE" WAS AND FOUND it fascinating that he was Bill Williams's brother.

"What color is the pickup?" Lara asked Stetson.

"It is a muddy grey, just like about a hundred other pickups around here."

"Do me a favor, Jim, and look at the middle of the hood, and let me know if it has a big dent in it or if it is stove in."

"I should do this because…?"

"Because when I was running from some guys who were after me in the forest, I ran up and over the hood of a pickup, and it went crunch as my foot hit it. It isn't a likely place for a traffic ding so it might be what you guys in the enforcement biz call a clue."

"Shall I call you when I have looked?"

"Don't bother. I will be back out there by tomorrow afternoon."

———◆———

PIOTR SJOLUND, DIRECTOR OF THE PORTLAND ART Museum, and his colleague and expert on Russian art,

Sonya Tompkins, arrived at the Left Coast Cultural Center to find two guys in logger boots and ball caps lounging in chairs at the edge of the parking lot. As they approached, Piotr thought they were Duane Hanson sculptures because they were so lifelike yet immobile. They stayed that way as the two walked past them to the front doors, where they were met by Bradley and Lester, the two marshals.

"Is that a Duane Hanson sculpture out there?"

"Who is Duane Hanson?"

"He is a very well-known artist who sculpts figures that look like real people, warts and all, except they are made of resin, and they don't move."

"Those guys don't move. They don't talk, as far as we know, and they don't do anything else, but they are alive, we are pretty sure of that."

"Fooled me and I run a museum. I'm Piotr, and this is Sonya. I think Juan is expecting us."

Juan had assembled all of the center's Russian avant-garde works, including paintings, watercolors, drawings, and ink or paint on paper. There were a couple of ceramics, too. Together they constituted a shitload. In the vernacular of weights and measures, a carrion-can is more than a gut-bucket. A dumpster-lump is more than a carrion-can and a shitload is more than any of those. In other words, a lot.

Sonya dove in while Piotr and Juan got acquainted. The period she had deconstructed in her doctoral thesis was the 1920s and '30s in the Soviet Union when Stalin was hammering the modernists, and most of them were either underground (alive and hiding) or underground (executed and buried). When the Soviet Union fell apart a few years back, all sorts of modernist (avant-garde means about the same) work started reappearing. Since these works had been hidden and since most of the artists were dead, it was fertile ground for fakes, and there were—what is the denomination above a shitload? It could be a butt—that is 126 gallons…well, anyway—a lot of fakes running around. Definitely more fakes on the market than legitimate works that could be traced to a Kandinsky, a Malevich, a Lissitzky, a Romanovich.

The Cultural Center had very few records after Piper Williams had cleaned out the offices, but for some reason, she had left, on the floor no less, a file that contained some acquisition documents. Sonya looked at that first. Most of the letters of authentication were from Sergei Ashkenazy. One or two from the same "art advisor" would not arouse suspicion, but all of them?

The next badge of fraud was that many of the "sellers" were "collectors" who wished to remain anonymous. Yes, rich people often didn't want to advertise, but still… suspicious. And the descriptions of works was sufficiently breathless as to also be suspect: "An artwork, like a precious relic recovered from a long-forgotten shipwreck…" Time to let the art speak for itself.

She grouped the works by artist. She was at something of a disadvantage since she didn't have a laboratory with x-ray, infrared, ultraviolet, and chemical analysis to depend on. But one could learn a lot just by looking. Her mentor, Professor Denton Milano, had taught her to look at the brushwork, the colors, the composition, and the surface. (Lots of modernists slathered on the paint, and the *craquelure*—that is, the tiny cracks and checks in the paint—often disclosed age). But most of all, he said, just LOOK at the piece, and your brain will tell you the truth if you have immersed yourself in the work of this artist thoroughly enough to be part of his family.

She was not a rookie at this business. She knew that some purveyors of fakes claimed to be experts and collectors in their own right and asserted that they had obtained the works from "an Italian nobleman, and communist, who had purchased them on the black market in the Soviet Union thirty years ago." The purveyor would claim: "*l'expert, c'est moi.*" And give a Gallic shrug that invited no rejoinder. Except it was 100% bullshit.

She had been approached, as she was researching her thesis, by an art advisor who promised to quote her (thus establishing her bona fides as an expert) if she would agree to include a reference to one of his works for sale (and a picture of it, of course) in her manuscript, provided it was published.

Self-authenticating authentication.

When she had all the works by Lissitzky together, they were facially similar, but the brushwork, the color choices, the composition, and the feel were remarkably like the works attributed to Goncharova, Kandinsky, and Malevich. This was, she concluded, a steaming pile of fakes, and probably all fakes created by the same artist, albeit an artist of substantial talent, since he or she could emulate multiple styles.

"HERE IS WHAT I KNOW SO FAR," SONYA SAID TO JUAN, Piotr, Lester (who was especially attentive), and Bradley. "There is a bunch of stuff here that is attributed to an artist who may not even have existed. Nina Kogan is the signature on these three works, and she died, supposedly of starvation during the siege of Leningrad in 1942. Her works, the lore goes, were sent abroad by friends after her death. Nobody can describe her or even verify if she was real. It is a forger's dream.

"These two here, that claim to be by Kazimir Malevich, were probably copied from a catalogue of an exhibition somewhere because the colors are not vibrant enough, the brushwork is the same throughout, rather than the exuberant riffs like those of an improvising jazz musician, and—and this is the big *AND*—they flat out couldn't have afforded him even if pieces such as this were on the market. I mean we are talking millions.

"There are three things that lend credibility to the provenance of an artwork. One is if it came from a family member or the estate of the artist, the second is if there is something like a photograph of the artist with the painting in the background, and the third is if the work was exhibited during the artist's lifetime. All of those are tough to come by with Russian avant-garde, but none of the stuff here has any of it.

"I would like, if it is possible, to take several of these paintings back with us to Portland, and do the chemical and scientific analysis, but I can give you a 95% certain opinion today that none, I mean none of the Russian modernist art here, is legitimate."

The two Hanson sculptures in the parking lot didn't move as Piotr and Sonya left, each with a painting in hand.

CHAPTER 20

Prepare your useless mind.

———◆———

Running, or trying to, with your hands behind your back is a bitch. Your balance is all messed up without your arms swinging with each stride, and when you trip and fall, you break the fall with your chin. OUCH.

How to get up? Bertie rolled around, trying this and that with no success until he finally scooched up with his back to a tree and pushed himself up with his legs, scraping the skin on his arms on the rough bark. Each time he fell, Bertie uttered an f-bomb. Soon the crows, like a Greek chorus, picked up the chant:

F-bomb.

Caw, caw, caw, caw.

F-bomb.

Caw, caw, caw, caw. They were laughing at Bertie.

He decided to walk; walk carefully. If he fell down where there were no trees, he could lie there until a cougar came along and ate him.

Having spent much of his life wandering around the forest, his sense of direction was reliable, but his mind did not immediately form a plan. Planning had never been Bertie's strong suit. In fact, if he had been able, or even interested, in parsing out what was his strong suit, the exercise would have befuddled a mind nimbler than his.

As he was stumbling along not thinking, he came to a road. He knew this road because he had plowed it through himself with a D-8 Cat. He also knew that while the direction to his left went upward, that was just an upslope of a small valley, and the route out of here to a main road was left.

Walking on the road was much easier. The thing was, all those cops and sheriffs might be on the road, too. Surely they had realized he had kicked the van's back doors open by now. What to do?

He stumbled on.

The crows were chanting contrapuntally—caw, caw, caw, caw—first from one side of the road and then answered from the other. Bertie's f-bombs provided a pedal tone each time he tripped on a rock or a bump.

He was getting close to a road with traffic. He could hear it. He made his way, carefully, into the trees and took a peek. Three or four vehicles, including two pickups, were randomly parked, like maybe the transportation of forest workers who might be going home at the end of the day's work? What the hell. He chose the pickup without a tailgate 'cause that was the one he could get into. He rotated his body around, kind of like the Fosbury Flop high jumpers do, and thrust his body into the bed, then snake-wiggled up so he was against the back of the cab. There he rested, and there he awoke as a door slammed and the pickup started to move. And he started to slide.

Oh, Momma.

He managed to brace his legs against the side of the bed and push with his hands behind his back as a kind of brake. If he had been facing the other way, he would have slid out the minute the truck accelerated. He relaxed a little bit as the truck maintained speed, but if he slid out now, at 60 mph, he would be a dead bouncer along the asphalt.

———————◆———————

BY THE TIME LARA'S PLANE LANDED IN PORTLAND, PIOTR and Sonya were back from the Cultural Center, so she went directly to the Portland Art Museum on the downtown's South Park Blocks. It consisted of a red brick main building connected by a sculpture garden to what had been a Masonic Temple constructed of yellowish masonry. She went into the lobby, asked for Piotr, and was escorted to his office.

"Aah, the famous Lara Cole," he said, getting up from his desk and shaking her hand. "Your prior escapades have been the talk of the profession, and now you seem to be on to another adventure. Pleasure to meet you."

Lara was used to this kind of attention, which she did not appreciate, but had learned to ignore. "Pleasure to meet you, Piotr." Then, to short-circuit the inevitable question about her past icon capers, she said, "Have you had a chance to look at the artworks at the Left Coast Cultural Center?"

"I have, or rather Sonya has. She is in the lab right now looking at a couple of pieces we borrowed. Let me get her up here," and he picked up the phone.

In Lara's mind, all persons named Sonya were blond and Nordic. This one wasn't. She had dark hair, dark-rimmed glasses, a nice smile, and a no-nonsense manner. She strode in, wordlessly shook Lara's hand, and began:

"X-rays show that one of the two we brought back, the Romanovich, has another painting under it. It is a fake, pure and simple. On the one that is signed by the phantom Nina Kogan, the microscope shows flecks of acrylic in the titanium white, and that material wasn't available when it was supposedly painted. I could go further, but these are both fakes, and I would bet my reputation that everything else in their collection is too."

"Nice to meet you," said Lara.

<hr />

THE ROSEBURG OFFICE OF DISTRICT ATTORNEY JIM Stetson was busier than usual after the Big Bust. Roseburg, previously famous for the big blast that ruined the downtown, now had another moniker, not that the Chamber of Commerce was particularly thrilled to be known as weed-town. Jim didn't exactly have a staff of young and ambitious trial lawyers. He had a secretary, who preferred to be called a "legal assistant," who told him to get his own damn coffee. A waitress she was not. And he had an intern, a law student at the U of Oregon in Eugene, who made it down to Roseburg when she could.

But so far, he didn't have anyone to charge or try because all of the weed-workers had skedaddled and Bertie Williams was still at large. The land on which the weed was growing belonged to Williams Lumber, and Bill, the pope, swore that he knew nothing about such nefarious activities. Williams Lumber could be fined by various state and county environmental agencies, and he, as DA, could perhaps seek forfeiture, but one had to tread carefully where the pope was concerned.

Meanwhile, Stetson was entertaining Lara, Juan, Marcia Stone (aka Stoney, who had all six-foot-plus of herself

wrapped around Juan in a coitally suggestive manner), and
Piotr and Sonya from the Portland Art Museum.

"This is a conference room, not a bedroom, for heaven's
sake, Juan, behave yourself," said Lara.

To this, Juan, only unwrapping himself partially, said:

"The art the Left Coast Center bought

Was not authentically wrought.

The pieces are crap,

This could cause a flap,

'til the crooks all around here are caught."

"Jesus, Stoney, can't you do anything to stop him?"
asked Lara.

Stoney just smiled.

THE MEETING WAS LARA'S IDEA, SO SHE WENT FIRST:
"Sonya has established to my satisfaction that much, maybe
all, of the collection of the Left Coast Cultural Center is
not legitimate. That is, the works are copies or forgeries of
famous artists."

"I agree," said Piotr.

"What this means is that large sums of money have
flowed through the Cultural Center, purportedly to pay
for these fakes, but what really may be going on is a money
laundering scheme for the proceeds of the marijuana that
you have found growing."

"How would that work?" Stetson asked.

"If Bertie was selling to whoever was his dealer, he had
to do something with the money—in cash, no doubt," Lara
replied. "That cash could go to Williams Lumber, or it could
go directly to the Cultural Center, and Williams Lumber

could simply be credited with an unspecified contribution. Then the center buys fake art from an 'art advisor' who takes a fee, but kicks back the bulk of the money to somebody, and my guess is that's Piper Williams or Piper and Bill, and then Piper spends it."

"I'm not liking this one bit," Stetson said.

"But I am," Stoney said.

"Why?" the DA asked.

"Because we have her deposition tomorrow and it is a civil case, so she can take the Fifth Amendment and not answer, but we can tell a jury about it and they will dump all over her, and we can levy on her house and the assets of the Cultural Center," Stoney replied. "This could be a real ball-buster."

"What proof do we have, beyond your speculation, that Piper, let alone Bill, have any knowledge or participation in this 'scheme' you have conjured up?" Stetson asked.

"Piper took all the records of the Cultural Center and she will do something with them, either cook up phony books or play stupid," Juan said. "But Williams Lumber has got to have a donation record of money going to the Cultural Center. They wouldn't have shown it as cash because there is no way they could explain where that kind of cash came from."

"Unless she takes the Fifth on every question, she has to tell us about this 'art advisor' she dealt with, and we can track him down and make him spill his guts," Stoney concluded.

They wouldn't, though, because Sergei (Sam) Ashkenazy was out of the country.

Permanently.

CHAPTER 21

Turkey vultures circling announce that something is dead.

T he pickup stopped, the door slammed, and Bertie yelled, "Help me." He had blood on his chin and down the front of his shirt and all over his arms and back. He was a mess.

The driver at first jumped back and then cautiously approached the pickup bed and looked in.

"Bertie?"

"I can't see. Who is it?"

"It's Roger. What the hell happened to you, and why are you in the back of my pickup?"

"I'll explain later. Would you please cut this goddamned plastic so my arms are free. I can't feel my hands at all."

Roger pulled out his jackknife and cut the zip tie. Bertie moved his arms around gingerly, as if they might just fall off, and then pushed himself up to look at Roger.

"Thanks. You got any water?"

Roger helped him out of the pickup bed and to a hose in the yard. He stood there, not particularly curious, because Bertie was a chronic fuckup, and if what Bertie had done involved the law, he, Roger, didn't want any part of it.

Roger said, "I don't need to know a thing, Bertie. The town is that direction. I never saw you today."

Bertie started walking.

It was dark, and it took him a long time to get to town, primarily because he dove into the ditch every time he heard a car coming, and when he got to the Roseburg outskirts, he had to duck through yards and up back streets until he came to Williams Lumber. There was a hole in the perimeter fence and a shed he had used before. He was hungry as hell. He needed to get cleaned up, get some food, and decide what to do.

Clothes would not be a problem. There were plenty of work clothes around the mill, and if he was careful and timed it right, he could take a shower in the crew's changing room as long as he didn't do it during shift changes. Maybe he could also swipe somebody's lunch pail.

He did all that and felt better. He still had the zip tie bracelets on each wrist. He sat in the shed and tried to think. It was hard because sometimes his brain was just too loud, and his thoughts kept spinning around like clothes in a dryer.

First he thought he should call Piper. While his groin liked the idea, his head told him, in a muddled way, that if she really cared about him, she would have told him to get the hell out of there after they saw the plane. If he threw himself upon the mercy of Piper, she might just kick him overboard.

Next he thought about his big brother, Bill. They had never been close, but Bill had given him a job and bailed him out of minor scrapes with the law before. Bill was big on keeping the doodoo off the family name. But did Bill know about the weed farm? Piper had always told him not to mention it to Bill—and he hadn't. Was this just being careful, or was it Piper's deal alone?

He could turn himself in. No, he wasn't going to do that. He had been in jail a few times and didn't like it at all. Anyway, Piper could finger him for that other stuff he had done, or at least let the cops know, and then he would really be up shit creek.

He could steal a car and beat feet out of here. All the money he had was what was in his wallet—about fifty bucks. He knew enough not to use a credit card if he was on the run.

He could live in the forest. He could trap and shoot deer, if only he had a rifle, and he could probably steal enough stuff from houses or farms on the forest edge to get by. But for how long? He didn't want to be a mountain man for the rest of his life. This was hurting his head. He lay down on the floor, took off his boots, used them for a pillow, and went to sleep.

The next morning he was awakened by voices of mill workers doing stuff near the shed. Sooner or later someone would find him here, and then he would have to tell them who he was, and then something would happen, and it would probably be bad.

He put on his boots, whizzed through the cracks in the floor in the corner, peeked out cautiously, and snuck out through the fence the way he had come in. He didn't have a plan. He wandered until he found himself in the yard of the Victorian mansion. He crawled into some bushes to think. He hung around until late enough in the morning that he was sure Bill had gone to work, and then he went to the big oaken door and rang.

If Imelda Marcos could do it, Piper thought, she could, too. Being rich was an atmospheric sort of thing, and the higher you got, the higher you got. She didn't need the marijuana to use for herself, but it was a way to get big money with very little effort. And that made her high indeed.

Ferdinand Marcos had stolen at least $10 billion, if you believed the papers. And Imelda, who didn't know any more about art than she did, had bought all these Van Goghs and Monets (or was it Manets—she thought there were two of them with similar names) and Picassos. That was first-rate stuff. Piper was envious. And what happened? Ferdy fled in 1986, but Imelda ran for president, and while she lost, she was still serving in the legislature and everybody loved her. Of course, the Philippines was different from here. Maybe.

She wasn't much worried about her deposition tomorrow. She had all the records, but they weren't going to get them. She first thought about dummying up a bunch of stuff, but that would be tricky and she would have to involve someone else, and so far, she had avoided anyone else knowing, except for two others, and one had been taken care of, but the other was in the wind and needed to be managed.

So she had her butler burn them, every last scrap of paper they had retrieved from the Cultural Center. They demanded records. They could rub it in their hair. The computers were already in the landfill.

The doorbell rang.

The butler knocked quietly on the doorframe of her study.

Should he let Bertie come in?

THE DEPOSITION RESUMED IN JUDGE LEIGHTON CARVer's courtroom in Eugene as before. The same cast of characters was there, as before. The US attorney asked that the witness be sworn. This time Piper Williams was dressed in a tightly cut man's suit with a slender necktie, and a skirt slit up to the hipbone, topped off with a pillbox hat with a black veil. The veil was down covering her eyes, nose, mouth, and resting lightly on her chin.

US attorney: "Please stand and be sworn."

Piper Williams: "We went through that last time; we don't need to do it again."

US attorney: "Ms. Court Reporter, please administer the oath."

She did: "You do solemnly swear, or affirm, that the testimony you are about to give is the truth, the whole truth and nothing but the truth, so help you God?"

Williams: "I don't practice religion."

US attorney: "Do you swear to tell the truth or not?"

Williams: "We did this before; why are you making it so difficult, sir?"

US attorney: "I am going to get the judge and ask him to administer the oath," which he did.

Judge Carver: "Madam, please stand and raise your right hand."

She stood.

Judge Carver: "Would you please lift the veil so I can see your face while I administer the oath?"

Williams: "That would violate religious principles."

US attorney: "You just said a moment ago that you don't practice religion."

Williams: "That doesn't change the religion."

Judge: "Madam, let me make this clear; you have been summoned to give testimony. You are represented by counsel here. To give testimony, you must first swear to tell the truth. If you are not prepared to do that, I am prepared to hold you in contempt. Please take a moment and consult with your attorney, and then tell me what you choose to do."

Brief recess. Consultation with first-class attorney.

Back on the record.

Judge: "Please stand, lift your veil, and raise your right hand: You do solemnly swear..."

Williams: "It's Okay, Judge, you don't have to go through the whole litany."

Judge: "I am losing patience with you. Do as I instruct you. Do it now."

Piper sits down, crosses her legs, opens her purse, takes out a cigarette, and says: "I will not be bullied."

Judge (to the US marshal): "Please relieve this woman of the cigarette, take her to the jail, and book her in. Madam, I hereby hold you in contempt for your willful failure to abide by the rules of this court. We will reconvene at this time tomorrow. You may then purge the contempt by complying with the obligations of a witness. Adjourned."

The marshal promptly returned to the judge's chambers to report that the jail in Eugene was full, whereupon the judge ordered that she be transported to Roseburg where she was lodged in the same not-so-commodious cell that had housed Lara.

---♦---

BILL WILLIAMS WAS ON THE HORN, LIVID. HE SCREAMED at Senators Andy and Fred. They listened, were sympathetic, let him vent, and then said, in as mealy-mouthed, subservient, content-deprived politico-speak they could muster, that judges were in a different part of the Constitution, and the separation of powers…Bill had hung up before the second of them had finished rambling.

He had been instrumental in getting these same self-important senators to persuade the president to nominate his old boyhood chum to the Ninth Circuit Court of Appeals. He called his judge friend and told him to call Judge Carver and read him the riot act and get his goddamned wife out of the goddamned jail. Boyhood-judge-friend said he would make a call but warned that he had little authority without a formal appeal being filed, and… well, anyway, he would make a call.

He did. Talked to Judge Carver, who read him the exchange with Piper. Judge Carver had had it transcribed and pinned to the wall of his chambers. The appellate judge called Bill back and said, "No dice."

Bill had no choice but to go to the jail and talk to his goddamned wife.

CHAPTER 22

The problem with slime is that it doesn't wash off.

———◆———

Roseburg had a bicycle cop. He just liked to ride his bike, a mountain bike with 27 gears, and nubby tires, and a carrier on the back with a pouch for cop gear. He didn't have a siren or emergency lights, but he had a radio and good eyesight, and the kids loved it when he pulled up and chatted with them. Turns out he was the most effective guy on the force (okay, there were a couple of women, but they were called guys—only so much you could do to change embedded culture). The chief wished some more of his fat-assed, donut-quaffing officers would get on bikes and out of their sagging-seated patrol cars.

So, on the previous day, as he cycled by the Victorian mansion, the bike cop saw somebody waiting at the door. He just got a glimpse because by the time he had turned around, the person was gone. He got off his bike and looked around, but didn't see anybody, so he rang the bell. The butler came to the door, and the cop asked if anyone had been loitering around. The butler (what a pretentious load of horseshit he was) said he hadn't seen anyone and began to close the door, which pissed off the cop who didn't like being door-faced. He asked a few more questions and got evasive answers and then asked: "Have you seen Bertie Williams around here? Every cop in the county is looking for him." The butler said no. Lying scum-sucker.

"I DON'T THINK THAT IS ENOUGH TO CONVINCE A JUDGE that we have probable cause for a search," said DA Stetson. What he thought but didn't say to the chief and the bike cop, was that he didn't have the balls to ask for a search warrant for the pope's mansion.

PIPER CONCLUDED THAT SHE HAD NO CHOICE BUT TO let the now most bothersome Bertie in. It would be inconvenient to have him here, but he needed to be managed. The butler showed Bertie to the basement changing room next to the pool. Bill never came down there, but Bertie was instructed to keep quiet, stay put, and remain dumb. Piper didn't have a plan yet. She had to think. She instructed the butler to keep an eye on Bertie, see that he was fed, maybe give him some magazines to occupy his mind, such as it was, and she would let him, the butler, know about next steps.

Then Piper went to her deposition, and thence to jail without passing go.

THE BUTLER HAD SERVED PIPER, AND ALMOST INCIDEN-tally, Bill, for a decade. Bill, he knew, was so laser focused on his business, and pulling strings with the rich and famous, that he paid next to no attention to what went on in his mansion or for that matter with his wife. Piper, on the other hand, was an open book. She was greedy, impulsive, self-absorbed, vain, and jealous.

They got on famously because he was loyal, subservient, compliant, and ready to whip out whatever she desired whenever the spirit moved her. He did what he was told. Neither possessed what you would call a conscience.

Now, however, with Piper in jail and no instructions to guide him, but with a realization that the intellectually challenged Bertie knew a lot of information that would be inconvenient, and with the mansion mostly empty since Bill was driving back and forth to Eugene, the butler determined it was time to give himself some orders. He surely did not want to join Piper in jail—that was not the kind of service he performed.

He took Bertie a nice piece of cake the cook had whipped up the day before. He didn't know why the cook did that because Piper never ate any and Bill did only occasionally, and it was up to him to polish off most of it. Maybe she had the hots for him. It was possible.

Bertie liked the cake and the butler asked casually if he, Bertie, would like to go for a swim.

Bertie said he didn't know how to swim. The butler offered to show him some strokes. "Come over here next to the water, not too close. Now bend over like this and move your arms like this." He demonstrated. He moved Bertie's torso from behind, assisting him in the two-arm-flail. Then he tossed Bertie into the pool in one fluid motion. He picked up the long aluminum pole with a screen on the end and cracked Bertie smartly on the head each time he bobbed up.

It took less than two minutes.

—————————•—————————

Jail did nothing to contrite-ize Piper. She told Bill she would damn well tell those lawyers and the tight-assed judge to stick it. He pleaded with her. She buttoned her lip. He begged. She demurred. He cajoled. She persisted. In the end, he gave up. He wanted to be in the courtroom in Eugene the next morning, but he knew this was one situation where he wouldn't be giving the orders. He would follow the procession when the marshals brought the jail van to fetch her.

By this time the press had gotten word of Piper's courtroom antics, and although press cameras weren't allowed in the courtroom during ordinary trials, this was a deposition that was being videotaped as well as taken down in stenotype. What fun.

Piper had on, not the swanky outfit of yesterday, but an ill-fitting orange jail jumpsuit and flip-flops. The marshal brought her in, plopped her down in the witness chair, and went to tell the judge they were ready. This time he came out in his robe—his authority garment—and called the proceedings to order. He stood before Piper and asked her if she was prepared to take the oath and testify.

She did not respond.

He asked again.

She looked him straight in the eye and held her peace.

The judge told her that if she had anything to say for herself, she should say it now.

"Further the deponent sayeth not," wrote the court reporter.

"We will do this every morning for as long as it takes," said the judge. "Take her back to jail." Back she went to the jail van. Back she went to Roseburg. Back she went to the not-too-commodious cell.

———————◆—·—·————

Disappointed that they had learned nothing from Piper, Stoney and Lara were talking in the hall outside the courtroom when Lara's face went pale and she froze in midsentence. Stoney turned to see a tall, fair-haired man in a business suit and carrying a briefcase walking toward them. Schooled in the signs of disabling infatuation she poked Lara in the ribs mouthing: "Do something."

Lara, displaying all the fruits of years of higher education, said, "Oh, hi."

He stopped.

They looked at each other.

Stoney looked at one and then the other and said, "You can either kiss or tell the other your name. What is it going to be?"

They exchanged names, not that she was now called David and he Lara, but they still were just standing there looking at each other.

Stoney said, "Jesus, people, get a life," and stalked off.

David: "You have a case here?"

Lara: "I was going to watch a deposition, but it didn't happen."

David: "The Roseburg museum thing?"

Lara: "Yes."

David: "So you have some free time?"

Lara: "I guess."

And so it went, agonizing step by agonizing step. Dogs can tell if it is time to play after a couple of sniffs. Humans let all sorts of big-brained impediments spoil the fun.

———•—•———

THE PRESS REPORTS WERE MIXED. KEEP IN MIND, BILL owned the Roseburg paper. Some said the judge was being a bully. After all, Piper hadn't been accused of anything. She was only being asked to give testimony. And hadn't the Williamses been generous public citizens giving to multiple worthy causes?

Others speculated that Piper must have a lot to hide since she was going to such great lengths to avoid testifying. And then the speculations orbited off into everything from child pornography to alien abduction. There was, after all, a certain segment of the population that would believe anything and another group that was easily and mindlessly entertained.

The more spectacular news, however, was that Bertie Williams's body had turned up in the local cemetery. He still had the yellow zip ties on each wrist, and a dangling piece where it had been cut. He had abrasions on his chin and what looked like dents in his head.

He was dumped about where the casket holding Linda McKenzie had been found.

———•—•———

THE CORONER REPORTED THAT BERTIE HAD DROWNED. The Umpqua River was nearby, and had, over the years, claimed its share of nonswimmers, but Bertie's lungs had water with chlorine in them, and that meant swimming pool. The season was such that outdoor pools were typically drained or covered for the winter. The only indoor pool, other than the YMCA that anyone knew about was in the Victorian mansion. Stetson knew this, but he didn't want to. He fiddle-farted around for as long as he could, but Stoney and Lara and the US attorney were all on his case. Finally, he gave in and drafted the affidavit that resulted in a search warrant for the home of the pope.

The butler answered the door. He told the US marshals and Douglas County sheriff's deputies that neither of the Williamses were home, and therefore they couldn't come in. They pushed him aside and went in, laying the warrant on a table in the foyer. They told the butler to keep his hands to himself, keep the hell out of the way, sit in a chair, and don't move.

Lara followed the cops in. Having a non-cop as part of a search is a colossally bad idea. She could potentially contaminate the scene, could get hurt if there were rough stuff, and really, had no business being there. But there she was. It was Lara being Lara.

She wandered around the house. It was large but not grand; pretentious but not stylish; flashy but not sophisticated. Money didn't buy taste. There were several of the probably fake Russian avant-garde pieces hanging on the walls, and Lara suggested that they be tagged and taken as evidence—of what she was not entirely sure.

The pool area, a primary focus of the search, yielded little, although they did take the aluminum pole with the wire strainer basket. It was slightly bent.

What Lara expected to find, and of which there was no trace, were the records that Piper and the butler had taken from the Cultural Center. She wandered back to where the butler was sulking and took a chair.

She didn't say anything. Just sat.

Silence can be terribly disquieting. She sat some more. No words.

He squirmed. Finally, he said, "Why are you here?"

She turned as if she had just noticed that he was sitting there and said, "This is a waste of time, don't you think? I am just here to keep an eye on these guys, but there are too many of them."

He grunted. It is hard to pull off a grunt with an English accent.

She quieted some more.

He said, "You with the DA?"

"No."

"Reporter?"

"No."

"What, then?"

"Just watching."

"What for?"

"I don't trust these guys."

"Oh," he said.

More quiet.

"You know Mrs. Williams?"

Lara just smiled.

"She gonna get out of jail?" (English accent had disappeared).

Lara shook her head in a direction that could have been read as either yes or no. She smiled some more.

Quiet.

He slid down in his chair with his legs outstretched, leaned his head back, and closed his eyes.

Lara studied him. Kept quiet.

Finally he started and said, "I gotta get out of here," but he didn't go anywhere.

Lara did some more quiet. She had been raised in Catholic schools—she could be the queen of quiet.

He got up, walked around the room as if he had never seen it before. He stopped in front of the fireplace and peered in, kicked at an ash on the hearth with the toe of his shoe, came back, and flopped down in his chair. "Gotta get out of here."

* * *

OUTSIDE, JIM STETSON WAS TAKING OFF HIS BODY ARMOR. He had a six-gun strapped to his hip. Cowboy. He asked Lara, "Learn anything from the butler?"

"As a matter of fact, I did."

"What?"

"He's nervous. Wants to get out of here. He may be a runner. That's one. Next, he cares about Mrs. Williams. There might be some extracurriculars going on there, and third, you might want to check out the ashes in the fireplace in the big ugly room in which we were sitting."

"He told you all that?"

"All I did was be quiet and observe him—you know, like people in law enforcement don't."

He flashed her a quizzical look, put his ballistic vest back on, and went into the mansion.

CHAPTER 23

Lay some unction on me.

N othing.
Nothing is exactly what was happening at the Left Coast Cultural Center. The two logger-guards sat, Bradley read, and Lester spent his time looking at the art. He was fascinated, even if most of these pieces weren't by whom they were purported to be, they still intrigued him, made him think.

The marshals were called down to Roseburg to toss the Victorian mansion. After that, they were back on the non-job of guarding, but that wasn't going to last long, since Uncle Sam was getting tired of picking up the bill for the center's security.

The search warrant for the Victorian mansion was duly returned (reported) with the catalogued items including some artwork, a bent pole, some dirty dishes found in the pool area, and a bucket full of ashes from the fireplace in the big ugly room. The ashes contained enough legible unburned corners to conclude that they were records of the Left Coast Cultural Center. The dishes had been sent to the lab for fingerprint processing.

No intact records were found, but multiple empty bankers boxes told the tale.

THE GARAGE OF THE MANSION CONTAINED THREE VEHI-
cles: the block long Mercedes, a Range Rover SUV, and
an ancient Volkswagen Rabbit. Upon warning from Lara
that the butler was likely to flee, they had installed track-
ing devices on the VW Rabbit and the Range Rover. The
Mercedes was too conspicuous for a getaway car. The Range
Rover was Bill's car, and it, too, was sufficiently dissimilar to
most of the clap-trap vehicles in Roseburg, that if one were
trying not to be noticed, the Rabbit was the ticket.

Sure enough, the beeper on the Rabbit started trans-
mitting at 10 p.m. It only beeped for about five minutes
and then it stopped. The butler, got out, rang the buzzer
for the jail, was let in, and stuck a very big revolver under
the nose of the deputy who had answered the buzzer. The
butler whacked him upside the head, and he fell. The piece
of shit jailer, hearing the commotion, was under his desk
yelling, "The keys are on the desk; the keys are on the desk."

The butler took the keys, unlocked Piper's cell, and led
her out of the jail. He took off, insofar as a Rabbit can do
that, with Piper riding shotgun. They got about three blocks
when sheriff's cars were all over them like ugly on an ape.
The butler knew he was had and stopped, whereupon Piper
jumped out waiving her arms and screaming she had been
abducted. Oh, thank god you deputies are here, and similar
soap opera recitals of the maiden in distress. She was good.

PIPER ENDED UP BACK IN JAIL, AS DID THE BUTLER, BUT
he was going to stay awhile, whereas she…well, this called
for a conference. And another parade of the jail wagon back
to Eugene. That is why Bill and Piper, and their first-class
attorney Haskins were sitting in Judge Carver's courtroom
along with Douglas County DA Stetson, the US attorney,
Lara, as representative of the National Endowment for the
Arts, Juan Oropallo, as representative of the state attorney
general, and Stoney, just because she wanted to be there. The
judge didn't have his robe on, but he had called the meeting because he didn't know what to do with the recalcitrant
Mrs. Williams, who now was maybe an abduction victim,
maybe an escapee.

As this was an informal negotiating session, the court
reporter was not present. The judge started out by recount-
ing what they knew:

- The records of the Cultural Center had been taken
  by Mrs. Williams and apparently destroyed.
- While the parties could use that information in a
  trial for damages, it didn't make much sense to continue to hold her as a reluctant witness since there
  wasn't much to talk about without the records.
- She had left the jail. Whether that was voluntary or
  involuntary was yet to be proved.
- The Cultural Center apparently was full of fake art,
  if the information he had been given by Lara was
  correct.
- There was a marijuana business, some of the proceeds of which had made it to the Cultural Center,
  but it was unclear where the money went after that.

- The Cultural Center owed the NEA its money back.
- The state attorney general could close the center for multiple violations of state law.
- They had two dead people on their hands.

"That's not all the ingredients in this rancid salad, but let's stop there and hear whether anybody has an idea how to digest this mess."

First-class attorney Haskins: "Judge, you have got to let Mrs. Williams out of jail. She has been through enough, and there is no reason to continue to hold her on a contempt charge."

Judge: "That's not real clear to me, counselor, but let's leave that issue aside for a minute."

Juan: "Judge, we need to get at the bank records of the Cultural Center and find out if it still has money. There are state fines, and the NEA should get its money back."

Judge: "Where did the Cultural Center do its banking, Mrs. Williams?"

No answer.

He looked at her. She looked back, imperious even in her jail jumpsuit and flip-flops.

Haskins: "I have instructed her not to speak, Your Honor."

Judge: "Well, that's swell."

Bill Williams: "I don't know anything about the finances of the Cultural Center, but I would be willing to guarantee any debts it might be responsible for, if we can settle on a figure for that."

Judge: "There is the question of governance. I understand there isn't a board of trustees or a staff."

Nobody said anything. The judge looked around, then said: "Why don't those of you here talk among yourselves and see if you can come back to me with a suggestion about how all the issues here could be settled. Don't worry about the murders. Those don't 'settle.'"

With that he retreated to his chambers.

<hr />

STONEY SAID, "LADY, I DON'T KNOW WHERE YOU GET OFF destroying the records of the Cultural Center, but if it were up to me, I would sue you for every nickel you have because you are screwin' with some good people here, and I don't like it."

Juan put his hand on her arm, but she wasn't done. "Why don't you tell us how the young lady—what was her name?"

Juan said, "Linda McKenzie."

"Yeah, Linda McKenzie," Stoney continued. "How did she happen to get killed? My guess, and I don't really think it is a guess, is that she knew you were cooking the books of the center to cover your marijuana business and probably the profits from the sale of the center's artworks. How about I spend the next couple of months building a case on that and then turn it over to my friendly DA here, and you spend the next thirty years in the slammer?"

Piper just looked at her. Didn't speak, but her glabella, the space between her eyebrows, was twitching. Bill put a restraining arm on her shoulder, and her first-class lawyer, Haskins, did the how dare you bit. Everyone started screaming at everyone else.

Then DA Stetson said something about how they weren't supposed to concern themselves with the murders now, and shouldn't we talk about the future of the Cultural Center?

"What future?" Juan said. "There is no board of trustees except perhaps for Mrs. Williams, and I think we can all agree that she has disqualified herself, so who is there to run the place?"

Stetson said, "There are good people here in Roseburg and the surrounding area, and some of them have been associated with the Cultural Center. As I understand it, they quit when Piper fired the last director. Maybe they could be persuaded to come back."

"Come back to what?" Lara said. "The collection of which they were so proud is a farce. The books have been cooked. The NEA wants its money back and probably a dozen donors are standing in line to sue. The AG wants to jerk their nonprofit status. Give me a minute, and I can probably think of six more reasons why the place is untenable."

Nobody said anything.

The US attorney, who had been quiet up to now, said, "We have been having discussions with a number of the indigenous tribes in this area about reparations from the federal government. The issues are complex, from fishing rights to burial objects to encroachment on sacred grounds. One of the things we have found is that the different nations don't have a common agenda. So I am thinking, since the Cultural Center is already in existence, and there is a wonderful building out there, and any new birth would have to be completely different, why not try to get some of the local tribes to run it."

"You mean as a casino?"

"No, casinos are indeed the revenge of the Native American; but no, I mean as a Cultural Center emphasizing the Native cultures of this area."

"There is a collection of wonderful materials that I have examined, very briefly," said Lara. "But the owner wouldn't come near the Cultural Center."

"I think I know who you mean," said Stetson, "but if the center were completely reconstituted would that person think again?"

"She is a smelly, crazy old bitch, and the stuff she has isn't worth a shit," said Piper, regaining her voice. Her first-class lawyer told her to shut up.

Bill Williams said, "I would be willing to consider funding such a project for a limited period of time, in exchange for some assurances that the US attorney and the DA would agree not to prosecute for any real or perceived breaches of the law up to this point."

"You are talking about a get out of jail free card for you and your wife?" said Stetson.

"Precisely."

CHAPTER 24

What virtue is there in not weeping?

Meanwhile, in the Roseburg jail, the butler was calculating his chances. He had been really stupid trying to break Piper out of jail. Whether it was loyalty or lust, it was bound to fail. He didn't know about the negotiations going on in the judge's Eugene courtroom, but he knew he had information that would be most useful to the prosecution if Piper were indicted.

He also knew that she could pin a whole raft of nasties on him if she needed to save her ass.

She wouldn't hesitate.

So far, nobody had come to lend a helping hand—no lawyer hired by the Williamses, no words about how they appreciated his years of service, no thanks for all the dirty work he had done without complaint. What he had right now to help him out was jack shit. That and a phony English accent.

THE MEETING BROKE UP SO THE VARIOUS SIDES COULD chat among themselves. The judge said Piper was going back to jail. For her, he had not a lick of compassion. She had proved herself a cosmic pain in the sacroiliac.

Bill needed to have a heart to heart, or maybe more properly a wallet to purse, talk with Piper, but jail was hardly the place for it. He pleaded with the judge to let them use his jury room before they hauled Piper back to jail in Roseburg. Okay. Forty-five minutes, and then back she goes.

When the door shut and while Bill was looking around the room—there couldn't possibly be cameras or listening devices in a jury room—Piper started in with her usual razzmatazz. Bill screamed, "Shut up!"

She was dumbfounded. He had never talked to her like that, so thorough was the crotch-whipping she had administered. She began to cry. When all else fails, crying usually does the trick.

"Stop crying," he yelled. She did. Turned it off like the tap in a sink. "I don't want to know details, just the broad brush here so I can see how deep this hole is. Just listen to my questions and don't talk until I ask you to."

She nodded. Did a couple of obligatory sniffs and sobs, and tried her best to look contrite.

"How long has the marijuana business been going on? More than a couple of years?"

He looked at her. She nodded.

"Was Bertie always involved?"

She nodded.

"The money basically came to you, have I got that right?"

Yup.

"So the folks out there are correct that the stuff in the museum is schlock and that you knew it was schlock. It was just to launder the money, right?"

A poor little forlorn waif, she was not. She nodded. He didn't know the half of it.

"Here is the big question. How could you possibly have thought it was all right to involve the lumber company in dummying up false contributions to cover the laundry. Don't you see that that could bring down the whole empire? That could get me indicted, too. That has to be the stupidest, the greediest, the most selfish…"

She got up and tried to embrace him. He shoved her back into her chair.

"You had to have help inside the company. Those false contributions had to be authorized by somebody and it sure as hell wasn't me. Who?"

Here was the leverage Piper had been looking for. She didn't answer.

"Who is it?"

"You told me not to speak."

"I am telling you to speak, goddammit, WHO?"

"That person will have to be eliminated," she said.

"WHAT! I can't believe I heard that. Did you murder Bertie?"

"No, I didn't murder Bertie, but he could have put us all in jail, so it is just as well he is gone."

Bill was—what is the most explosive adjective? That is what he was. Had he lived with this woman so blindly for 25 years and not even suspected what she was capable of?

"What about that other girl from the museum that got killed. Do you know anything about that?"

She smiled. Smiled. Can you even believe it? This woman, my wife, is a monster.

The marshal knocked on the door and yelled, "Time's up."

"And one other thing you need to think about, my dear husband: our butler, who is now in jail, is a bomb that needs to be defused, and you are the smart guy who can figure out how to do it. Ta-ta," and she walked out with a little wave, flip-flops slapping the floor.

STETSON ASKED LARA IF SHE WANTED TO LOOK AT THE hood of Bertie's pickup. It was in the impound lot as evidence. Bertie was dead, so he wouldn't have to be prosecuted, but they still had multiple crimes swirling around including the murder of Linda McKenzie, the growers of the marijuana, and the killer(s) of Bertie.

Sure enough, the middle of the hood was stove in. "Here is where my shoe hit the fender as I leaped up, scared out of my wits, and in the middle of the hood is a shoe print that will match my running shoes," Lara said. The prints were covered with dust and were fairly indistinct, but Stetson called a photographer to preserve them. "There were two guys, one on the four-wheeler, and one next to the pickup, who probably was Bertie, although I couldn't identify him, and, I guess, never will have to.

"Linda McKenzie was running, or walking, same as I was. Do you suppose she came upon the marijuana fields, and that got her killed?"

"That could get her killed, but so could uncovering the money laundering through the Cultural Center," Stetson said. "If we could find out who was on the four-wheeler, we might be able to squeeze him for some answers."

"How do you find him?"

"No idea."

Lara was seated—that is, after the objects piled on the couch were piled on top of other objects piled on the floor—with a cup of tea, talking to Maud, aka the Crazy Lady, who was anything but.

"It doesn't surprise me in the least that that Williams lady was up to no good. She struck me as a total phony. She just swept in here, turned up her already turned up nose at my collection, offered me a fraction of what it is worth as if she were donating to a charity, and cursed me when I wouldn't sell," said Maud.

"She didn't impress the judge with her antics, but her husband has offered to throw some money at the problem if it will make it go away," said Lara.

"What? To buy a little justice?"

"Sounds like it, doesn't it? But the problem exists throughout the art world. People who have made large contributions, who have endowed symphonies, built museums, and donated art have sometimes made their money on the backs of slave labor, or have sold products that harm the public, or have otherwise been less than model citizens. So what do we do, since we are beggars who exist on the crumbs from the table? If we had to have a cleanliness test before we accepted any donation, we would all be out of business in a week," said Lara.

"Have you heard of the Diogenes Syndrome?" Maud asked.

"You mean the guy with the lantern who went around looking for the last honest man?" Lara replied.

"Same mythological name, but in this case the syndrome is used to refer to old people who surround themselves with junk, like books they have never read, or in my case, artwork that lots of smart folks don't know the value of. They say I am a crazy lady who collects colored rags and throws away food, but the food I collect is more nourishing than anything at the finest restaurant.

"But," Maud continued, "the government may be getting smarter, or maybe it is just that the collective conscience of a nation that has treated Native people despicably is finally beginning to tickle, because the Smithsonian has just opened a museum honoring the American Indian, and maybe they will want my collection.

"Some of the art I have is unbelievably sophisticated. It is not just the use of natural materials, but the Northwest tribes created works in four dimensions. By the way, your National Endowment published a book titled "Toward Civilization"; they had no idea what the word means."

"It's not my Endowment," said Lara, because she pretty much agreed. "What if the tribes around here wanted to have a local showplace, somewhere that their art could be honored and displayed, and where they could get together and celebrate their cultures?"

"Great idea. How would that ever happen?" asked Maud.

"Bill Williams has suggested he is willing to buy his wife out of trouble. My thought is that since the Cultural Center's collection is disreputable, and the only way it could reopen would be as a joke that everyone could laugh at, like "Come see the museum of fakes," maybe he would be willing to fund a new not-for-profit that would include your collection and be a real Cultural Center for the tribes."

"You know that the tribes don't all speak with the same voice; they have their own opinions and different agendas."

"Educate me," said Lara.

"There are nine federally recognized tribes around here. Let's see if I can remember them all," Maud said. "There is the Burns Paiute Tribe to the east of here. They got stomped upon by most of the other tribes that came their way; then there is the Coquille Tribe west of here (it is pronounced Coke-well, by the way). Cow Creek is just down I-5 in Canyonville where they have a casino—pretty good food, I am told; then there is the Confederated Tribes of Coos, Lower Umpqua and Siuslaw farther down the coast. How many is that?"

"Four if a confederated tribe only counts as one."

"I have got to think locations here, because they are spread around the state. There is Grande Ronde and Klamath, and Umatilla—that's farther north—and Siletz—that's north and west, and Warm Springs north of Madras off of Highway 395. Got 'em all," Maud chortled.

"Who would be a decision-maker about something like this?"

"I have a few ideas," said Maud. "Let me exercise my crazy wiles."

CHAPTER 25

"Mystical" and "undefinable" are synonyms.

———◆———

"The ball is in our court," said Stetson. "Bill Williams has offered to buy their way out of this mess, and we could go on screwing around trying to get testimony and money, or we could just take the money and forget about the screwing around."

"That is as practical as it is chickenshit," said Stoney, never one to put frosting on a turd.

Juan said, "Getting testimony, without records and witnesses is going to be colossally hard. We could try this case on circumstantial evidence and lose."

"Since I am not a trial lawyer," said Lara, "and I don't have to parade my win/loss record..."

"Never heard of such a thing," said Stetson.

"...why don't we talk about what we might accomplish through an agreement with Bill Williams?"

They did, and here were some of the negotiating points:

- Williams agrees to fund Cultural Center for 10 years, at $500,000 per year.

- The money is escrowed in an irrevocable trust (all

$5 million) so he can't change his mind.

- Neither Piper nor Bill can have anything to do with the center forever.

- A new board of trustees will be appointed by some-body—not the Williamses.

- The NEA will get its money back (hopefully there is a Cultural Center bank account somewhere), and Piper will have to make full disclosure—no more stonewalling.

- Try to get the tribes to agree to sponsor the center to display/champion their cultures.

- All art, whether real or fake taken from the center by Piper—or anyone else we can find—will be returned.

- Williams Lumber cleans up the marijuana fields and promises to patrol all lands they own/manage to prevent further crops.

- Both Williamses apologize publicly for being slime bags.

- Any release of liability will not affect murder charges or gathering of evidence for such charge(s).

After they had noodled some more and couldn't remember what they were forgetting, Lara told them about her conversation with Maud. Maud didn't give any indication of how long it would take her to talk with whomever she was going to talk, but she warned that it might take awhile. What she said was something to the effect that white eyes build in right angles; Native Americans in circles. "A museum," she said, "is a process, not just a place."

THE FIRST-CLASS LAWYER, HASKINS, WAS BACK BEFORE Judge Carver pleading for Piper's release from the slammer. The judge asked how the negotiations were going. Haskins demurred, saying he had not been asked to participate. The judge told him to go back to Bill Williams and tell him that if he wanted to get his wife out of jail before the second coming, he had best make a deal, because until then, she wasn't going anywhere.

This news prompted Bill to tell Haskins to contact the other side and get another meeting ASAP. Haskins was also invited to participate, but he had no illusions that his client was interested in his advice.

The "other side" was thrilled to receive the invitation for another meeting. In negotiations, two rules are immutable: the party that talks the most gives up the most; and, any sign you are anxious is like dropping an anvil on your foot.

The same parties as before were present, with the addition of the first-class lawyer, Haskins, and Stoney's dog, a big white Samoyed named Whitey (a joke, sort of). Stoney still had no standing to be there except that she was Stoney, and what did it hurt to have a dog there anyway? Judge Carver looked at the dog, shook his head, welcomed them all to his courtroom, and told them to get on with the negotiating.

Everybody sat around the table, except for Whitey who was lying at Stoney's feet. Everybody was studying notepads, busy drinking coffee, or pawing through a briefcase. Nobody talked. Finally Bill Williams said, "I made an offer to put some money on the table. It is your turn."

"How much?" Stoney asked.

She annoyed him. That was exactly her intent.

"Oh no, I am not going to bid against myself. What is your offer?"

Silence. It was Piper's game, but anyone could play it.

"I wasn't here for the last meeting. What money, and what was it to be for?" Haskins asked.

Silence. Lots of tabletop staring.

"I offered to finance part of the Cultural Center's programs, or whatever, to get the place back on its feet," Bill said.

"How much?" Stoney again. Lara thought Stoney was a real pistol and was glad to let her do the shooting.

Bill had been toying with some Thompson seedless grapes in a bowl on the table, and he let fly with one that whizzed by Stoney's ear. Whitey got up to go sniff it.

Speechless silence. None of the court-types had ever been to a food fight during negotiations.

Stoney stooped down and picked up the grape from the floor, looked at it, popped it into her mouth, and said, "Missed."

The room cracked up. Even Bill laughed, shook his head, and muttered, "Sorry."

For an icebreaker, it couldn't be beat.

———◆———

LARA READ THE LIST OF DEMANDS THEY HAD WORKED out. Haskins asked if she had a copy. She handed her sheet to him. Haskins suggested they break up to discuss privately. The jury room was still available, and he and Bill and Piper filed in there. Whitey got up and walked in right behind them.

They closed the door.

"Whitey loves everybody," said Lara.

"That sure as hell proves it," said Stoney.

———————

MAUD MET LARA AT THE TAVERN IN SALISH TO REPORT back on her conversations with the Indians. She was spry, and thirsty. She sat down and ordered a gin—not a martini, just gin in the rocks. That's what she ordered: gin in the rocks. She was dressed in a kind of kaftan-thing, flowing yet suggestive, a batik-flower-child-native-up-yours garment that said, well, "Up yours."

"She squeezed Lara's hand until it hurt, dispensed with the preliminary pleasantries, and let fly, only occasionally pausing to attend to her gin.

"First thing we have to remember is that each tribal government is a sovereign nation, so think as though we are dealing with the United Nations, with all of its dysfunction, rather than a couple of people who could say yes or no.

"Second is that none of these nations are going to forget for a moment the traumas colonialization has visited upon them. They signed treaties that were misrepresented, and which they could not read, and weren't worth the paper they were on anyway either because the Senate never ratified them or because the United States ignored them whenever it was convenient.

"Third is that these tribal sovereigns don't speak with a unified voice and have different cultures, teachings, beliefs, healing practices, and forms of governance, not to mention languages, art forms, and diets. But one thing they do have in common, thanks again to colonialism, is alcoholism.

They also have a cultural grief, kind of like soldiers who have battle-induced post-traumatic stress disorder—PTSD—from loss of communities, children that have been taken away and "re-educated," loss of land, self-determination, freedom, and cultural practices."

She raised her hand for another gin.

"Next, and don't try to keep count—after another gin I won't be able to either—is that what we call civilization is a distraction from a unity with the natural world. For us of the Western world, our senses have shriveled as our hubris has grown. For them it is a quest to recapture the mind of the wolf, if you get my meaning. Their artists are calling on mystical forces. They are neither ahead nor behind their times; they are of their time. They are of nature and are trying to live in harmony with the natural world. They are remembering the future.

"Next, and I am enjoying this, you are the best audience I have had since I was sitting in my house talking to myself," and she gave Lara's hand another bone-crushing squeeze, "they are probably not going to want to own a museum or cultural center or whatever because they don't own the sky or the river or the birds or the fields. They are, at least some of them, however, flush with money from their casinos, and they have proved to be quite generous in giving to nonprofit entities of which they approve.

"Finally, and this isn't all, but I am up for one more gin, and after that you will have to help me get back to my house: what you call this new place will matter. The process of naming can have significant spiritual meaning and may influence community beliefs which in turn could affect the success or failure of the whole project. So don't think you can just pick a name, throw up a couple of tipis and call it good.

"Well, actually, I do have some more steam in my boiler: some southwest Indians were weaving yucca and willow into blankets and clothing and sandals thousands of years before Christ. They were cultivating cotton and using their prayers and dances and stories for blessing and cleansing the earth. If they sign on to your project. No, that's not right. If they agree to be a part of this project, it will be to reclaim their truth."

She sat back, glugged down the last of the gin, and waived her hand around in the air for another. "Don't expect an answer right away, and if you do get one it is likely to be equivocal. Whoever is running this new outfit is going to have to earn their trust."

"Oh, and another thing: they don't necessarily trust each other. Planting a hatchet in the skull of an enemy is part of the deal."

With that she sat back and savored her gin in ice.

Lara helped her home and tucked her in. As Lara was leaving Maud thanked her for the conversation.

I didn't say a word, thought Lara.

CHAPTER 26

How many spin cycles does it take to launder the truth?

P iper Williams would never enjoy being in jail. But it did have some of the same features as home. She didn't have a butler, but she did have a jailer, the same piece of shit guy Stoney had ordered around, and ordering around was a game Piper had invented. She got him to bring her all sorts of unauthorized items, including sleepwear and blankets from the Victorian mansion. Dressed in the sleepwear, she could give the jailer discreet peeks. Her food was delivered from her own cook. And when the cook left, she could carry messages so that Piper was not cut off from her minions in the world of the free. The butler was locked up in another part of the jail, but the piece of shit jailer was happy to convey messages back and forth. And so it went.

One outside minion was particularly important to Piper because he was the source of all sorts of information about the doings of none other than her own husband. This information was not salacious, but financial. Money was what motivated Piper, and this particular minion, sitting as he was on the board of Williams Lumber, could provide all sorts of financial information that Piper craved and that Bill, as blind as a husband could be, never shared with her.

The minion was also the one who dummied up the "contributions" from Williams Lumber to the Cultural Center to help launder the marijuana profits. He had helped Bertie in the past and was beyond suspicion because he wore cork boots and suspenders, the sure sign of a dullard. He was also the one who worked with the tree rustlers.

Piper had a special project for him. It would not only eliminate (the government word was extreme rendition) a major problem in her life but would hopefully shut him up so he would not have to be extremely renditioned himself. Getting shivved in most prisons was commonplace; the Douglas County jail didn't have that kind of clientele. How he did it was up to him, but she made it clear that he had to do it while she was still in jail, and thus beyond suspicion.

The piece of shit jailer found her newly eliminated butler swinging by the neck from a ceiling pipe. He had apparently knocked himself out since he had a nasty lump on his head. Poor fellow never did have a name.

————◆————

IN THE HOURS AND DAYS THAT PIPER WAS PULLING THE puppet strings from jail, the others, all lesser players in her megalomaniacal world, were back at the negotiating table. They all wanted to get this thing done. Amazing what a flying grape and a white dog can do. Stoney assured them that while Whitey's hearing was acute, he could not talk and thus had disclosed no private exchanges from the money side.

Lara told them of her conversation with Maud, and that while the idea of a Center for Native American Culture was the goal, it would take time and nurturing to come to fruition. Stetson said he estimated the profits from the marijuana sales to be north of $5 million, tax free, of course.

Stoney opined that the scumbags (some of whom were sitting at the table) should be prosecuted and strung up by their thumbs. That was not helpful.

Bill Williams said he wasn't going to write a blank check and be on the hook for expenses nobody could, at this point, calculate. The US attorney pointed out, perhaps unnecessarily, that Mrs. Williams was going back to jail and was not likely to get out until they had a deal.

Whitey maintained his neutrality, first lying at Stoney's feet and then wagging over to be petted by Piper, who apparently liked dogs.

They broke for lunch.

FOOD AND A LITTLE TIME CAN DO WONDERS FOR NEGO-tiations. The deal, which still had to be written up and approved by the Williamses' attorney Haskins, DA Stetson, and the US attorney for language, but which was going to be drafted by Stoney since she knew that the purveyor of language had the home court advantage, had these points:

- Williams will escrow $5,250,000 to be distributed $750,000 per year to a not-for-profit that would take over and control what was now the Cultural Center.

- The title to the building and all of its contents would be transferred to that new organization.

- The Williamses, and anyone on their behalf, would have nothing whatsoever to do with the new entity.

- The trustees of the new entity would be chosen in a manner to be determined with the consent and oversight of Judge Carver or his successor.

- The National Endowment for the Arts would get its money back from the current assets of the Cultural Center, but if none were recoverable, Williams would make the payment of $125,000, which could be considered a contribution for tax purposes.

- Any and all art or other objects, records, or stuff (a legal term of art) in possession of the Williamses would be returned forthwith.

- Williams Lumber would clean up and sanitize all marijuana fields, and would patrol all of its land holdings, and those held by Williams personally, to prevent any further illegal cultivation.

- Bill Williams, Piper Williams, and Williams Lumber would not be prosecuted for any non-capital crime or cause of action related to or arising from any of the facts herein. Whoa…!

- No apologies.

- If at the end of seven years no entity had succeeded the Cultural Center, all moneys remaining in escrow would be distributed to other not-for-profit entities as designated by the new trustees and approved by the judge.

Piper would presumably be let out of jail and her contempt purged when all parties assured the judge that a deal had been signed, sealed, and delivered.

The law shoves messes down the road and when the unresolved issues reappear, as they are bound to do, none of the people who did the shoving will be around to answer.

No further proof is needed for that proposition.

⎯⎯⎯•⎯⎯⎯

STETSON STILL HAD THREE MURDERS ON HIS HANDS. As to the murder of Linda McKenzie, Bertie was probably involved, but he was murder victim number two. There was a guy on a four-wheeler who chased Lara, but that doesn't make him a killer, and there was no way to identify him. (Deputy Pflug had obtained a job elsewhere and had erased Roseburg from his memory.)

So, no clues for Linda. Bertie drowned in the Victorian mansion pool. Probably. He could have had help drowning, and the prime suspect for that would be the butler, but the butler was dead and was probably murder victim number three since it is unlikely that he could have knocked himself out and then hung himself from a ceiling pipe with a bed sheet. As to who could have helped the butler commit suicide—while he was in jail, no less—Stetson had no clues. The piece of shit jailer was on duty, but asleep and didn't hear/see a thing.

He got fired.

Stetson had an election coming up, and if he wanted to be bored for four more years as district attorney, his lack of a culprit for three murders could become an issue. He and Bill Williams, who was still the pope, had not exactly become friendly during the negotiations, but at least the Williamses, both of them, now knew who he was. That could be good or bad.

Piper was out of jail, completely unrepentant—she was like the cat who jumps off the bookcase as it topples forward spilling contents all over the rug, and then looks back as if to say, "How did that happen?" She had hired a new butler. He was a guy both she and Bill knew because he had worked for Williams Lumber and was on their board. He told Bill he was too beat up physically to keep working in the woods. Bill introduced him to Piper.

She pretended they had never met.

RANDALL AT THE NEA WELCOMED LARA BACK TO WASHington. He was glad to have the money back and hoped that the press didn't have the energy to investigate what a bad decision it had been to give the grant in the first place.

"Randall," said Lara, "will you never learn? The press finds out about everything, and when their story comes out it will be 100% negative. This is your chance to be a hero. You retrieved the taxpayers' money. You are on top of your grant giving. You care not just about good art, but good government—fiscal responsibility. Get your press release ready and send it out today. Create the narrative."

Lara told him she would monitor the progress of the new board of trustees in getting some of the tribes on board. A number of the new trustees were enrolled tribal members, and perhaps they could help create a vision that would allow the new entity to prosper.

"And," she said, "if you ever ask me to do a site visit again, I will kill you."

But Lara did have another piece of unfinished business, namely the niggling memory of that singer/lawyer/studlybuns dude named David with whom she had had only a short, disjointed, content-free conversation over cold coffee, but whose electricity continued to light up her brain. What, if anything, could come of that?

CHAPTER 27

Our emotions know the truth.

———— ◆ ————

Lara, after being back in DC for a few days, called George Graham and said, "I am back, and I need to conjure up some dignity. Are you free for lunch?"

He wasn't, but suggested a better idea—come over for dinner, and Alma will cook us up some soul food, and you can pour out your restless heart. Restless heart—that is what he said, and she knew it was true. She couldn't stop beating herself up for agreeing—as if she had any say in the matter—to a deal whereby Bill Williams bought his wife out of multiple felonies.

She arrived at the Graham house in Cleveland Park, a nice, older section of DC, with a bottle of wine about which she had no knowledge other than that she liked the graphics on the label. He took the wine, she hugged both George and Alma, and he handed her a bourbon on the rocks.

"This is called Old Tub. I like the name, and it is better than Dickel and not as lethal as Maker's Mark. Tell me what you think."

Lara said, "If I have more than one I will probably dissolve into tears and embarrass myself further."

"Time for therapy," he said, taking the chair next to hers. Alma excused herself to look after the kitchen.

210

"First thing you have to understand," he said, "is that the law is not about justice; it is about finality. We solve our problems with imperfect solutions, but those solutions are almost always better than citizens shooting each other. Both you and I can attest to that from our unfortunate experience in Russia.

"The second is that law is meant to do one thing and morality another. When the law tries to make people behave according to standards that religion or some other moral source decrees, people rebel, like making the sale of liquor a crime or telling people whom they can love.

"And the third is that all of our actions are imperfect. We can always do better. We fail miserably even when we succeed. This is the source of built-in guilt that religion has so successfully exploited. What I value is that you have the courage to make mistakes.

"I could go on, but does any of that strike you as true?"

"It is all true," she said, "but none of it makes me feel any better. I feel as if I have been slimed, and I can't let go of the injustice of it all."

"If you believed in an afterlife," he said with a small twinkle, "you could take comfort that they would get poked in the fanny with Satan's trident."

"Nothing about my trips to Oregon had the least effect on my views about heaven and hell, but if the role of divinity is to ratify privileges, I want no part of it."

"You can keep beating yourself up, but, Sweetie, you aren't responsible for fixing all of the world's problems. I learned that a long time ago. I can do what I can do, and do it the best I can, and then it's time to come home to a loving household, have a drink, put up my feet, and think that there is a lot to like about this planet."

Lara nodded. He was wise, she knew. Then she said: "Sometimes I think—I wish—there were multiple gods—a god of mercy, a god of compassion, a god of justice—and these gods would inform our better selves to bring real love to our world. She sighed. If only…"

She stared into her glass, took a sip, and said, finally, "I like Dickel better."

They both laughed, which brought Alma from the kitchen to announce that dinner was served.

Dinner was wonderful as was the company of a loving household that was as close to family as Lara had ever known. The wine was on the better side of okay, and they laughed and talked and the therapy was exactly what Lara needed.

"You know," she said, "Oregon is a pretty interesting place. Scenery is beautiful, the state is pretty diverse with ocean and desert and mountains and rivers. We should do a road trip out there some time."

Alma said, "You think you could stand this big lunk talkin' about life to you for a whole trip?"

"I'd be willing to find out."

Made in the USA
Monee, IL
11 December 2023